TIME OF DEATH

DOOMED

josh anderson

EPIC
Press

Doomed
Time of Death: Book #2

Written by Josh Anderson

Copyright © 2016 by Abdo Consulting Group, Inc.

Published by EPIC Press™
PO Box 398166
Minneapolis, MN 55439

Cover design by Dorothy Toth
Images for cover art obtained from iStockPhoto.com
Edited by Ramey Temple

LIBRARY OF CONGRESS CATALOGING-IN-PUBLICATION DATA

Anderson, Josh.
Doomed / Josh Anderson.
p. cm. — (Time of death ; #2)
Summary: Kyle Cash comes back to an alternate version of his life barely recognizable to him. If he can, his next trip through the tunnel may give Kyle another chance to fix the past, and even a glimpse into his own future.
ISBN 978-1-68076-065-1 (hardcover)
1. Time travel—Fiction. 2. Traffic accidents—Fiction. 3. Life change events—Fiction. 4. Interpersonal relations—Fiction. 5. Conduct of life—Fiction. 6. Guilt—Fiction. 7. Self-acceptance—Fiction. 8. Young adult fiction. I. Title.
[Fic]—dc23
2015903987

To Dad,
My trusted first reader.
Now, and always . . .

CHAPTER 1

IT WAS HER FIRST TIME BEHIND THE WALLS OF A prison, and the blond woman with the violent past actually had to break *in* to get here.

She adjusted her black baseball cap, placing her silk blot down on the long table. She pulled the karambit blade from her front pocket and held it in her hand. It was a new one, a different brand than she was used to, but the mechanics of using the claw-like knife would always be the same. It was the weapon she was trained with, and for her money, a lot more effective in combat than a gun. She brought the knife close to her face and admired the virgin blade.

She blew her blond bangs away from her face. Out of the corner of her eye, through the metal grid covering the windows, she could see that the sky was giving its first hint of morning. *Hustle,* she thought. *Prisons wake up early.*

She grabbed the handle of the knife in her left fist and tried scratching into the stainless steel table. The blade just slid along without leaving a mark. It was no accident that a prison administration would choose tables for its cafeteria with slick, scratch-resistant surfaces.

The blond woman heard a truck backing up outside. If anything was being delivered, it meant staff would be here to receive it. It was entirely possible that cafeteria workers would be arriving soon to get a start on breakfast. Her plan was to be in and out in less than five minutes. *There's no way*, she thought, as she tried again to etch the first letter of her message into the table.

Using both hands, she put her whole body into it and was able to finish a reasonable "K," but she was fatigued from just doing that. As skilled as she was with a blade, this simple act of vandalism was proving to be more than she bargained for. Curves would be impossible, so her "C" wound up looking more like an incomplete diamond when she finished it a couple of minutes later. There was no way she'd be able to get a twelve-word message carved into the table before someone found her here. Twelve words was already short—about the length of the average Tweet—but she'd need to boil her message down further.

She gave it as much elbow grease as she could, carving out the rest of the abbreviated message. Finally, after ten minutes, she finished. *Not terrible*, she thought, given the challenge of the table's slick surface. It was readable, at least:

KC: NO CLASS—2/25/16

She hoped Kyle would recognize his initials. If he did, the two-word command would be unmistakable. At least she *hoped* it would.

The blond woman heard another noise. This

one was from inside the prison and it sounded close by. It wouldn't be long before she'd have to spill someone's blood, or worse, just so she could get back into the silk blot and get out of here.

Picking up the knife, she saw some metallic residue from the table on its sharp edge. She couldn't resist quickly licking each side of the blade clean. The tasteless grit in her mouth was a small price to pay for the exhilarating feeling of the sharp metal against her tongue. She spit the metallic dust onto the tile floor and closed the knife.

As she pulled the silk blot over her head, the blond woman enjoyed one last second of cool air and steeled herself for the warmth inside the time tunnel.

CHAPTER 2

OUT OF SIGHT, AROUND THE SIDE OF THE HOUSE, Kyle Cash—who had traveled through the time tunnel from 2016—watched his mother drive away. When a second silk blot appeared in his cell a few weeks after his first trip through the time tunnel, Kyle knew that this time, he had to take the risk of going back to the morning of the crash. He couldn't depend on his father alone to stop the tragedy on Banditt Drawbridge.

He tested the nail gun by shooting it into his mother's planter beside the back door. The projectile nicked her favorite rose bush before burying itself in the soil.

He picked up the first two-by-four plank of wood and nailed its right side, and then its left side, against the outside of the doorway, about head high. He nailed the next one across the doorway about six inches above the floor and then another around belly level. Finally, Kyle nailed a piece of wood between the highest one and the belly-level one. It only took him ten minutes to nail fifteen slats of wood across the front door—some straight, some at angles. There was no way his 2014 self could squeeze through and get out of the house, nor could Joe Stropoli, who was inside with Kyle.

At this point, Kyle from 2016 walked up to the front door of the house and did the same thing, nailing enough two-by-fours across so no one could possibly get out. Someone driving by might think the house had been condemned, especially after Kyle took the large wooden boards he'd bought at Home Depot the day before, and nailed them over every window except one on the downstairs of the house.

Once he covered that last one, there'd be no way anyone could get out of the house without possessing something like a saw—and Kyle knew there was no saw in his mother's house.

Kyle knocked on his mom's bedroom window and waited. He knocked harder. He'd gotten the signal that the 2014 version of himself was locked up in the bathroom, along with Joe, where they were smoking a blunt and taking tequila shots, just as they had always done on the morning of the bus crash. But still, 2016 Kyle was afraid something could've gone wrong. He knew how risky it was to chance an encounter with his younger self, but this was too important.

He was there to try again to stop the bus crash he'd caused which had killed twelve middle school students, their driver, and Kyle's best friend, Joe. Because Kyle had gotten high and drunk with Joe before causing the crash, he had been sentenced to eight years in prison for manslaughter.

His first trip back in time had been to 1998,

a time *before* Kyle was born. This was done in order to protect Kyle from meeting another version of himself, which would have catastrophic results. He learned this, in 1998, when he saw his cellmate Ochoa's head explode after he made eye contact with himself as an infant. On Kyle's visit to 1998, he had convinced his father, Sillow, to try to stop the bus crash from happening in 2014, but the plan had failed. A mysterious blonde woman in a black baseball cap showed up on the morning of the crash to stop Sillow and ensure that the crash tragically unfolded on March 13, 2014. Kyle had no idea who this woman was, or why she wanted the crash to take place exactly as it had the first time.

Now, here was Kyle, so close to his younger self that he could toss a baseball upstairs to him. He saw the blinds over his mother's downstairs window start to roll up and he couldn't help but wince, afraid something had gone wrong and that he would see his own face staring back at him through the window.

Kyle was relieved when his father pulled the window up, and started to climb through.

"You got the phones?" Kyle asked.

Sillow reached into the pocket of his jeans. "Right where you said they'd be."

"Time check?" Kyle said.

"Eight forty-six," Sillow answered.

"Thanks," Kyle said.

"Thank me when this works. I still can't believe I've done this whole thing before," Sillow said, referring to his attempt to stop the crash the last time. "This whole time travel thing makes my head hurt."

Sillow had no recollection of his earlier attempt to stop the crash because, like most people, he was living in a linear timestream. This day—March 13, 2014—hadn't happened for Sillow yet. Kyle only knew the result of their first attempt to change the past because he'd lived two years past today already.

After Sillow finished climbing outside, Kyle nailed the last board over his mother's bedroom window.

Kyle heard a banging noise around the side of the house. *Clunk . . . clunk . . . clunk . . .* "Are you sure they're still up in the bathroom?" Kyle asked. He walked around the house quickly, trying not to make much noise.

Sillow followed right behind him. "Thirty seconds ago, they were."

It was the blonde woman in the black cap again, the same one who'd been there when Kyle went back to 1998, and when Sillow tried to stop the crash in 2014. *Who is she?* Kyle wondered. She was wildly swinging his mother's snow shovel against the two-by-fours covering the front door. The shovel was plastic, and after a few hits it split, and she dropped it. She pounded her fist on one of the wooden boards and screamed out in frustration.

She didn't look any older than she had in 1998, so Kyle realized that she was traveling through time as well.

The woman turned, saw Kyle, and did a double take. "You came back here?" she screamed. "You can't do that!" She started down the steps and toward them, with a frantic look on her face. "You can't do that!"

Kyle was startled and started to step backwards. Sillow followed his lead.

The woman pulled a gun out of the back of her pants and pointed it toward them as she approached. She pulled a curved combat knife from a holster on her pants with her other hand.

"Shit," Sillow said. "You never said anything about guns. Shit, shit, shit!"

Kyle didn't say a word at first. He just pointed to a black disc attached to the side of the house. He showed the woman a small remote control in his hand. "You shoot, I hit the button," Kyle yelled. "The whole house blows up, including the people in it." There was no time for small measures now. It was dangerous enough to be here, and he had to make sure he succeeded. Even if that meant killing himself.

"You didn't say nothin' about explosives neither," Sillow whispered as the woman walked toward them. "If you blow your younger self up in there, what happens to the *you* who's standing right here?"

"No idea," Kyle answered. "But I bet I don't cause a bus crash in twenty-five minutes."

The woman locked eyes with Kyle and didn't look away as she got closer to them. There was something familiar about her face. She was probably in her thirties, beautiful, but with a hard look to her. "You can't be here!" she repeated.

Kyle held his hands in front of him. "I had no—"

"You *did* have a choice. You just made the wrong one," she said. "All it takes is a few seconds of eye contact with the other Kyle in there. Did you forget what happened to your friend?"

"Who are you?" Kyle asked her.

It took her a second to form an answer. Kyle could see that she was struggling with her words. "Right now, I'm your last warning. You need to get back into your silk blot, and home to 2016. Right. Now."

"Why do you want those kids to die?" Kyle asked. She was so familiar, but he couldn't figure it out. His photographic memory wasn't doing its job.

"We don't have time for this," she said. "Kyle, please. You need to go."

"So, I leave and you just make sure the crash happens same as it always does?" Kyle asked. "I need to know why."

"*Why* is not important right now. The details don't matter!" she said. "The result *will* always be the same. And the more you do to change the little stuff, the more chance of making things end up much worse. That's how it works, Kyle Cash. The big stuff is gonna happen, one way or the other."

The way she said his name . . . *It couldn't be. It doesn't make any sense*, he thought. *Allaire?*

"Why? How? Allaire? I can't even . . . " he said. "I can't leave until I stop this crash." The tears in her eyes confirmed it for him. Even with her eyes welling up, she looked tough and world-worn, with a couple of new scars that she didn't have as a teenager in 1998. "I can't believe it's you. If you're Allaire, then you risked seeing yourself in '98 too."

"I take that risk all the time, Kyle," she said. "I know what I'm doing. *You* need to go back to 2016. This isn't about us. This is about you making it out of today alive."

Kyle couldn't believe that the girl he'd fallen in love with and said goodbye to in 1998, which for him was only a few weeks ago, had become this woman in front of him. He had more questions for her than he could even begin to list.

"Seriously," Allaire said. "*That* Kyle is going to

call the cops, or find some other way out of that house, and you can't be here when he does."

Sillow held up the two cell phones. "They won't be callin' anyone."

"I'm sorry," Kyle said. "I have to see this through. If you want to stop me, shoot me."

"I could never do that," she said, putting the gun back in the waistband of her pants.

Kyle bit his lip in frustration. "But you'll let thirteen people—twelve kids!—just nosedive off of a bridge?"

"They're already dead," she said. "They might as well be. How about we *both* get on the next bus into Manhattan? Whether your plan works or not, you still need to get out of here. There's nothing more you can do here, but die."

Kyle looked at the house, boarded up like it was burnt out. Without seriously risking a run-in with his younger self, there really wasn't much more that he could do. "You'll stay here?" he asked Sillow.

"Hold onto their phones, and do what you can to keep either of them from getting into a car?"

"Yep," Sillow said. "Flight back to Jacksonville ain't 'til morning. I'll do everything I can until then." Kyle knew from the last time that his father could be trusted.

"Last time I went back, the crash happened fourteen minutes later than the original one," Kyle said to Allaire. "I can make a difference."

"Small details," she said, her tense face loosening up a bit. "Big picture is that we have to catch the bus."

Kyle looked at the house once more. He put his arms around his father, who tensed up for a second before hugging Kyle back.

"Does it hurt?" Sillow asked.

"What?" Kyle asked.

"Going through time."

Kyle broke the hug. "Nope. My head just feels a little weird when I get back."

"Bye, son," Sillow said.

Kyle started to walk away and then turned around as a thought occurred to him. "Hey, Dad . . . Whatever happens, make sure to come find me in 2016. Hopefully not back in prison. Okay?"

CHAPTER 3

MARCH 13, 2014

a few minutes later

"WHOSE CAR IS THIS?" KYLE ASKED ALLAIRE AS they pulled into the parking lot of the Flemming bus station.

"It's a rental," she answered. "I used to just steal one whenever I time weaved, but then I had to watch out for cops the whole time. Now, I just use the I-rent-they-find program."

"I rent, they find?" Kyle asked.

"Yeah, I rent the car with a fake name," she said. "And when I'm done with it, I leave it somewhere for them to find. And I just go back through my silk blot."

"Are they really made of silk?" Kyle asked. For

all of his recent experience with time travel, he was completely in the dark about how it all worked.

"Sort of," she answered. "The process of making a blot starts the same way as spinning silk."

Kyle opened the door to the bus depot and they joined the line of people waiting to buy tickets. "Did someone just accidentally discover time travel?"

"Time weaving," Allaire said. "Every time you go back, you weave a new timestream into the universe."

"What does that mean?" Kyle asked.

"That after you weave back, you're never returning to exactly the same world you left," she said. "Even the littlest thing you do in the past will have some effect and create a new timestream—a new version of time."

"So, you just follow guys like me around when we time weave and make sure—" Kyle asked.

"I try to keep things tidy," she said. "And fix things that get broken before they can destroy the future. Listen, there's so much I *can't* tell you. I wish I could, but I promise, the tunnel isn't an accident."

Kyle's brain was racing. "I need to know more . . . "

Allaire pulled the collar of his t-shirt and planted a kiss on Kyle's lips. "No more questions. Let's think about *us*. I've been time weaving for half my life. It's my past, not my future. I want to go back to 2016 together and make a life with you."

Kyle looked away. When he went back to 1998, there was a brief moment when he'd fallen for Allaire and matched her crazy-intense feelings, or at least matched them part of the way. But this was a different Allaire.

"You think I'm old and ugly now," she said. "I get it."

"It's not that at all," Kyle said. "We don't even know each other. I'm a juvenile delinquent. You're a time traveler. That's a lot to digest."

She put her hands on his cheeks. "I could *never*

not know you, Kyle Cash. Our connection is still there, same as always. I don't care if my body says I'm 35 years old and yours says it's 18—"

"Seventeen" he said. "For another month . . . But, according to you, when we get back to 2016, I'm going to be in prison. Not exactly the best starting point for a relationship."

"I'll wait for you," she said.

Allaire was beautiful—at any age—and maybe he would want something with her. She just made him feel like it was somehow predestined—like he didn't have a choice. And, after two years in prison, the last thing Kyle wanted was choice being taken away from him.

This woman who was now twice his age held Kyle's hand as they waited quietly on a bench for the call to board the bus. The wind swirled violently around the old, wooden bus depot.

"You're shivering," Kyle said, taking off the Columbia ski jacket they'd bought together sixteen years ago and laid it over her like a blanket. "The bus will be warmer."

Kyle sprung up when he saw that it was 9:02, eleven minutes before the last version of the bus crash occurred. Bus #17 would be on its way to Clinton Middle School right now.

Allaire had warned him that details might change, but the crash would still go off as it always had. So, even though it was early, Kyle kept his ear out for sirens. He remembered the deafening sound of the emergency vehicles arriving right after the crash as he hung upside down talking to Joe Stropoli's lifeless head, dangling alongside his.

She kissed him once more, and again he didn't give much effort on his end. She pulled away quickly this time.

Kyle turned and noticed an older woman a bench away giving them a disapproving look.

"It was simpler in '98," Allaire said.

"Because we were the same age?" Kyle asked.

"Not just that," she said. "There was no baggage then."

Kyle could barely concentrate on their conversation. He stood up suddenly. "Be right back."

Inside the bus depot, he found one of the few remaining pay phones in Flemming. He dropped a quarter into the slot. He had to know what was going on over at the house. He needed some hint of what was waiting for him on the other side of the time tunnel in 2016. Would he be a free man? Would the kids from the bus all be alive? He dialed his own phone number, hoping Sillow would answer.

Ring . . . ring . . . ring . . . Voicemail. Sillow probably didn't think it was safe to pick up 2014 Kyle's phone. Kyle hoped the reason was as simple as that, and that nothing had gone wrong.

The bus to New York was just starting to board as Kyle got back to Allaire. They took two seats toward the back. Kyle stared out the window, looking for any hint of the bus's fate only a few miles away on Banditt Drawbridge.

"Do you think there's any chance it worked? Stopping the crash?" Kyle asked.

She interlocked her fingers with his. Despite being preoccupied, Kyle liked the way it felt. "I'm sorry, Kyle. No matter what you do, those kids will never see March 14, 2014. Time doesn't just *let* itself be defeated. The crash *happened*. If someone told you it was possible to make that not so, then I'm sorry. They were wrong."

CHAPTER 4

MARCH 13, 2014

a few minutes earlier

SURE, JOE THOUGHT IT WAS STRANGE THAT SOME-
one had locked them in the bathroom and boarded
up Kyle's entire house during the twenty minutes
or so that they were upstairs. It was *very* weird, but
they'd searched the house and there was no one
inside, so they were safe. Joe wished Kyle would
knock it off with the screaming. He was blissfully
high, and a little drunk too. His friend was just
bumming him out.

Kyle's neighbors obviously weren't home.
Yelling, "Help!" over and over wasn't going to do
anything if no one was around to hear him. Joe
would've preferred to be stuck at *his* house, with

the snacks he liked and his PlayStation 3, but it wasn't the worst thing in the world to be at Kyle's. Bottom line, it wasn't Joe's problem, he thought to himself. *Probably some boyfriend of Kyle's mom getting a little crazy.*

He laid on Kyle's comfy green couch feeling pretty satisfied with himself. He felt like a total badass when he was able to shimmy his pocket knife into the doorjamb of Kyle's bathroom and get them out.

"Help!" Kyle screamed through the wooden boards again. "We're stuck in here!"

"At least whoever did this can't get in," Joe said. "Even if they wanted to."

Kyle looked at Joe and rolled his eyes. "Will you shut up, please?"

Joe pulled the tequila from his jacket pocket and sat up to take another drink. He started to put the bottle down on the coffee table when he saw there wasn't much left. They'd drank more than Joe realized they had. He emptied the rest of the bottle into his mouth—a huge five-swallow sip that almost made him gag.

"You're a fuckin' idiot, Joe," Kyle said. "*Think* about what's going on here. You're not fucking scared?"

Joe shook his head. "Dude, your mom is gonna be home in a few hours. We're not gonna rot in here," he said. A second later Joe thought about what he'd just said and couldn't remember whether he'd said it loudly, or just quietly to himself. "Is this about your fuckin' math test, bro?"

Joe took out his favorite Zippo—the one with the pot leaf drawn in the colors of the Jamaican flag. One day, he'd visit Jamaica, he thought. Smoke as much weed as he possibly could. Figure out a way to mail some home to himself. There had to be a way without getting caught.

"Please! Help us!" he heard Kyle scream again, his face pressed up against the boards blocking the front door of the house.

Just chill the fuck out, Joe thought to himself,

but he was done trying to convince Kyle. It was a lost cause.

Joe flicked the Zippo open and ran his thumb on the wheel, igniting the flame. Fire looked so cool when he was stoned. One day, he thought, he'd get a place in the woods and build a fire every single night. Maybe one day he'd have a wife and kids to join him. She'd get high with him, of course, except when she was pregnant. And he wouldn't hide it from the kids. The same way his parents didn't hide drinking.

"Help!" Kyle shrieked, running upstairs now. This time the scream startled Joe and got his heart racing. Suddenly, looking at the flame from the lighter in his hand, Joe got an idea. *I can get us out of here.*

Sillow wished he could help 2014 Kyle, even though he knew he was safe inside the boarded-up house. His son sounded scared, screaming through the wooden boards, pleading for help. But, Sillow just stood watching from the woods across the way. He reminded himself that the best way to keep his promise to help Kyle was to make sure he didn't get anywhere near that school bus this morning. He bounced up and down to keep warm. Florida had spoiled him, and this was the coldest weather he'd felt for a long time.

He pulled Kyle's iPhone from his pocket. *How the hell does my sixteen-year-old kid have a nicer phone than me?* he wondered to himself. He'd been working two jobs for the last decade or so—hospital all day, gas station three nights a week—and it killed him that he still couldn't get his family out of the hand-to-mouth cycle. The huge screen on the phone said there was a missed call from a Flemming area code three minutes ago. *Probably one of Kyle's buddies.*

When Sillow looked back at the house, he first thought he noticed some rolling fog, or maybe some dust getting kicked up by the wind. But then there was more smoke, and then more. Clearly, there was a fire in the house. The smoke was white, and it danced out between two of the boards covering the front door. Sillow's mind raced. There'd be no way out if the house really was on fire.

Sillow started to run toward the house, but thought about how the blond woman had shattered a heavy plastic snow shovel trying to break through one of the boards. He'd never get them out in time. He slid the arrow on the screen to unlock Kyle's phone and dialed 911. Whatever happened with the bus, he wasn't going to let his son die in there.

Kyle bounded down the stairs and saw Joe standing at the open front door. That was when he saw the smoke. "What the hell are you doing?"

"Getting us out of here," Joe answered, not even

turning to Kyle. "You sound like a bitch with all the screaming. You're givin' me a headache."

Kyle walked closer and saw that a few of the boards covering the front door were slowly burning. Joe was using his Zippo to try to ignite another one. "Stop, Joe! You're gonna burn my house down."

"Just trust me," Joe said. "The fire will weaken the boards and we'll be able to kick our way out of here."

"Seriously, stop it!" Kyle said.

"You wanted to get out of here so badly," Joe said, pointing to a board at eye level. "Just let me finish . . . Look, this one's almost halfway burnt." There were seven or eight small fires on the boards. None of the fire had spread to the doorway of the old house yet, but Kyle didn't want to see what would happen when it did.

Kyle ran to the kitchen and grabbed the two largest cups he could find. He filled them with water and walked quickly toward the door.

Joe turned to Kyle as he was coming. "No way,"

he said. "Just let me finish. This is totally gonna work." Before Kyle could toss the water at the door, Joe smacked one cup out of his hand, and grabbed the other, pouring it onto the floor at Kyle's feet. Then, he went back to trying to light another slat on fire.

Kyle reached out and grabbed Joe's wrist. He used his other hand now, and tried to pull it away from the doorway so he could get the Zippo out of his hand.

"Get the fuck off of me," Joe said, pulling his hand away.

"You're gonna burn the house down with us inside," Kyle pleaded. He realized he was dealing with "drunk Joe," who was a lot less chill than "high Joe." The tequila this morning was an unusual addition to their morning ritual, but Kyle hadn't thought much of it until now, when his friend was being dumber than he'd ever seen him before.

Joe pushed Kyle away and turned back to the door. Kyle could see the little fires were spreading even more. His heart raced. Joe was bigger than he was, and although they'd never had a physical altercation, Kyle was pretty sure he wouldn't be able to overpower his best friend.

"Joe—look at me. You are gonna fucking kill us," Kyle said. "You realize that?"

Joe pulled out the blunt now and lit it. "Stop being dramatic. You're being a pussy, dude."

Kyle knew he had to do something. *Couldn't Joe see all of these little fires spreading toward the wood of the doorway?* he thought to himself.

Kyle put both arms around Joe and tried to wrestle him away from the slats covering the doorway. The blunt fell from Joe's hand as both of their feet slid on the wet floor. Joe was laughing, but fighting at the same time. "Kyle, get the fuck off me. I am seriously going to fuck you up in minute."

Kyle ignored Joe. Using all of his weight, and the slick wood floor, he was able to twist Joe off his feet to the ground. If he could pin him down, maybe he could talk some sense into him.

"Joe!" Kyle screamed, pointing at the door. "No more fucking around. You're gonna burn the house down. We need to put this out."

Joe pushed Kyle off of him and stood up. He was no longer laughing. "You always think you're so smart, Mr. Honor Roll! You wanted to get out of here so bad, but you don't like this 'cause it's not your idea."

Joe started toward the door again, and from the ground, Kyle grabbed his left foot. "No, Joe!"

As Joe tried pulling his foot away from Kyle, his right foot slid out from under him and he fell toward the wet floor.

Kyle felt an initial sense of relief as Joe went down face first. But, then he cringed at the sound of Joe's head hitting the floor. It was a louder sound than Kyle would've expected.

Assuming Joe would be up and at it again in a second, Kyle ran back to the kitchen to get more water. This time he grabbed a huge metal salad bowl and filled it up. He raced back to the door, spilling water as he went, careful to slow down as he got to the giant puddle in front of the door.

When Kyle got back to the living room, Joe was still lying face down in the puddle, his head turned to the side and his eyes closed. Kyle hurled water from the bowl onto the door and managed to extinguish about half of the small fires.

Kyle figured Joe must've knocked himself out. He bent down and poked him in the arm. "Joe . . . Joe . . . Wake up."

Kyle bent his head down to look at Joe's face. His eyes were closed and there was no movement at all. He heard sirens outside. Then, Joe's body convulsed. Then, he convulsed again.

Kyle lifted one of Joe's eyelids, but there was no movement underneath. "Joe, come on! Get up! They're here to get us out." Kyle saw the blunt on the floor and grabbed it. He walked over to the couch and tossed it underneath. "Dude! Wake up!" he yelled.

It barely took thirty seconds for a couple of firemen to break through the door with their axes. The next couple of minutes were a blur to Kyle as more and more rescue workers came into the house. The firefighters quickly doused out the rest of the flames, while the EMTs focused on Joe.

The first time it occurred to Kyle that Joe might be really hurt was when he watched the firefighters turn him onto his back. His limp arm just swung across his body as they flipped him, sending his Zippo to the floor with a clang.

More and more emergency personnel streamed into the house. They tried CPR, then one of those things with the paddles to try to start his heart. By the time Kyle heard someone say it a few minutes later, he had an idea it was going in that direction.

"He's gone," a tall EMT said to the woman administering the paddles. Then he looked over at Kyle and quickly looked away. Kyle knew the police wouldn't be far behind the medics, especially with such a bizarre scene. Kyle wondered about the wooden boards. *Who boards up a house with people inside?*

"Time of Death, 9:13," one of the medics finally said. Kyle felt like he was watching a movie. Everything going on had an odd fog over it.

Kyle saw Joe's Zippo just lying on the ground next to his covered body. He wanted to grab it. It had lit so many of their blunts, joints, bowls and bongs over the years. Kyle had made fun of Joe for the Jamaican flag colors, even though he had two Bob Marley posters in his room himself. Joe treasured that lighter and it didn't seem right to Kyle that it was just lying there. He walked over and picked it up, giving his friend another look. Everything had happened so quickly. Kyle began to tear up as the reality of the situation hit him all at once.

"Can we tag him, bag him, and get out of here?" the tall EMT asked his colleague, a petite redhead.

"Or do we need to let the crime scene unit come through?"

The redhead gestured with her head toward Kyle, and stood up. "Damn straight they do. There's another kid here, no witnesses . . . Weird as fuck incident. I'll go check how close they are."

The tall EMT looked at Kyle, and then shuffled out behind the redhead.

Kyle walked to the doorway. He looked outside at the flashing lights of the two ambulances and the fire truck. Then he turned again to the bizarre scene in the house.

He wondered whether the police might blame him for this somehow. Then, that small thought became bigger.

He saw the redhead on her radio and knew the police would be here soon. Suddenly, Kyle's heart began racing. His knees felt weak. He imagined a reality in which the police blamed it all on him. *What the fuck is happening?* he wondered. The tears flowed harder and harder, fear heaped on top of his sadness.

Kyle was hyperventilating by the time he grabbed his keys from a hook next to the front door. He ran to his white Nissan Sentra. He needed to go somewhere and think about how he was going to explain everything to the police. He needed air. He left the front door open just as it had been.

Neither the redheaded EMT, nor her tall partner, noticed Kyle as he walked past them to his car. He turned over the ignition, threw it into reverse out of the driveway, and raced down the block. He didn't know where to go, so he drove toward school.

CHAPTER 5

ONCE 2016 KYLE REALIZED THAT ALLAIRE REALLY wasn't going to answer any more of his questions about time weaving, he gave in, and they made out for most of the bus ride from Flemming to Manhattan. The middle-aged man sitting across from them changed seats after fifteen minutes, getting up with a "*Pssshhhhh.*" It was unclear whether he was put off by their very public display, or their age difference—or both.

As they were getting close to the city, Kyle pulled away, but Allaire looked at him and purred. "I don't want to stop," she said. On one hand, it felt strange to Kyle to be making out with a grown woman. On the other, it didn't feel very different from when they'd been together in 1998.

A few minutes later, just as they were about to roll into the Port Authority bus terminal, Kyle's mind went back to the crash. "Tell me this wasn't all for nothing."

"There are desperate people out there who want certain things to be possible so badly," she answered. "I'm sorry."

"Myrna," Kyle said, referring to Etan Rachnowitz's older sister. She had provided Kyle with the silk blots he'd used both times he'd gone back.

"She got preyed on, Kyle," Allaire said. "Desperate people hear what they want to." Kyle could tell from the way she'd said it that maybe Allaire had fallen victim to hopefulness at some point too.

Allaire broke into his thoughts. "You're the apple

of my eye, Kyle Cash, but you are small potatoes when you go up against the force of time."

"I was supposed to do whatever it took to stop you from trying to mess with the past," she continued.

Kyle noticed something he hadn't before: she was wearing something that looked like a wedding ring on her left hand.

Allaire moved her right hand over her left. "I need you to be careful," she said. "Don't do anything to jeopardize our future please." She kissed him again, intensely and not in a way which gave him any choice in the matter. "Go back to prison, do your time, and I'll find you afterward."

She turned away and started up the aisle of the bus, clearly having decided that this was where they needed to part ways.

As he watched Allaire walk away, Kyle felt a pang of sadness and marveled at the fact that she'd managed to do it. Again.

At first, he thought of all her talk about them

being destined for each other sounded crazy. But by the end of their time together—only a couple of hours—again, he somehow found himself believing it too.

CHAPTER 6

FEBRUARY 22, 2016

two years later

JUST LIKE LAST TIME, WHEN KYLE FIRST EXITED the time tunnel and got back to his cell, his legs were too weak to hold him upright, and his mind was too foggy to know whether he'd failed or succeeded in his goal to stop the bus crash. He collapsed to the floor and pulled himself on to his bunk again.

This time, though, the weakness lasted only a couple of minutes. Physically, he felt like himself again only a few minutes after exiting the time tunnel. The different memories of the day of the bus crash assaulted his mind all at once, though, and Kyle needed to lay down and stuff his face inside a pillow to try to quiet his thoughts.

He peeked up at the clock on the wall and it was only a minute later than when he'd entered the silk blot. Kyle had lived two days in 2014 with hardly any time passing at all in the present.

Slowly, his mind began to process everything that had happened. Looking around, he spotted the list of the kids killed on the bus still on his wall. His folder full of newspaper clippings was still sitting on the small, metal desk at the foot of his bunk. It was clear that this cell was still Kyle's. He couldn't quite locate the memory of what had happened yet, but he knew Allaire had been right. He'd failed to stop the crash.

There were now a few different versions of the day of the crash, but whatever the result of his trip back to 2014 just now, this new version would be the only one that mattered—the only reality that Kyle could live in.

As he lay in his bunk, Kyle felt the new memory developing—a memory of having lived that day in 2014 from the perspective of his younger self became clear to him. He remembered wondering who blocked all of his doors and windows with wooden boards, Joe trying to burn the boards covering the door, trying to wrestle him away, and then Joe slipping on the water Kyle used to put out the fires. Kyle driving away before the police arrived . . . And then, the crash.

This memory was now melded with 2016 Kyle's memory. Yes, he remembered wondering who barricaded the doors. But he also remembered barricading the doors himself. These conflicting memories created both a fog and a clarity in Kyle's head that he had never experienced before. Remembering events no longer meant just stopping and thinking, it meant sorting through the various viewpoints that were all living in his head at the same time. Aside from living it in multiple timestreams, Kyle had literally lived that morning from two different perspectives. Sorting out his recollection of any event involving the day of the crash—even for someone whose memory had always been his greatest strength—was hard work. And it left Kyle with the unusual feeling of never quite being one-hundred percent confident with any of these memories.

By the time Kyle had enough of a handle on his memories to stand up and grab his folder of news clippings, he could see parts of the headlines in his head without even looking: ARSON . . . BIZARRE MURDER . . . TRAGIC CRASH . . . These were new headlines—different than the ones Kyle had known by heart since the original crash, but they were burned into his brain as well.

Kyle tried to calm himself by breathing deeply, but he felt regret deep in his stomach as this most recent reality became clearer and clearer to him. Kyle heard a tapping on the cell door and heard the lock turning over. He was relieved to have a reason to wait a moment before looking at the clippings in his folder, which he knew by now would verify this new reality. As the door was opening, he realized he'd left his silk blot on his bunk. He quickly folded it and stuck it behind the clippings in his folder—as good a spot as any to hide something in a ninety-six square foot cell.

Officer Radbourn, Kyle's favorite of the guards, opened the door and walked in, followed by another inmate Kyle didn't know, and Officer Gee, one of the less friendly of the guards at Stevenson Youth Correctional. The other inmate had a shaved head and was short, but very stocky. He was covered in tattoos all the way up his neck.

"How's it goin', Old Rad?" Kyle said, trying to muster enough energy for the usual friendly banter with Radbourn.

"What the fuck did you call me, inmate?" Radbourn answered, looking sharply into Kyle's eyes.

Kyle didn't know what to say. He'd seen Radbourn be firm before, but never this unfriendly. They'd talked hundreds of times before. "Old Rad" was everyone's favorite guard for a reason.

"Maybe it's all this time he's had by himself

without a cellie," Gee said to Radbourn. In the three weeks between Kyle's most recent trip back through time, and his first, when Ochoa was killed, the other bunk in his cell had remained empty.

Radbourn was clearly pissed. "Whaddaya think, you're on some fuckin' beach, smelling that salty ocean water, on some kind of vacation here, inmate? What am I, your waiter? 'Old Rad,' my ass. I'll crack your fucking skull if you ever call me that again."

"Only salty water I smell in here is some nasty-ass inmate sweat," Gee said with a smile.

Radbourn pulled the other inmate to his side by the arm. "Party's over, Cash. I'm sure it's been real comfy in here since that thug, Ochoa, up and disappeared," Kyle was surprised by Radbourn calling Ochoa a 'thug.' He was a tough guy, but he followed the rules, and Rad always liked him.

"Meet your *new* good-for-nothing cellmate, Leonard Pitkin," Radbourn continued. "Pitkin's just arrived at our little establishment, but he's not new to the system. Am I right, Pitkin? The two of you fuckin' deviants should get along great."

Leonard gave Kyle the world's quickest, most unfriendly handshake and the guards left. Kyle was shocked that Radbourn was suddenly so unfriendly. Was this something he'd caused by going back? Kyle wondered. Was this one of the ripples Allaire talked about?

As soon as the guards locked the door, Leonard walked over to Kyle's bunk and pushed down on the center of the mattress. He looked Kyle in the eyes, and didn't break eye contact as he walked over to his own mattress and pushed down on the center as well.

Then he walked right up to Kyle—so close he could smell Leonard's awful breath. "I like yours better."

Kyle thought about it for a second. Maybe Leonard needed this one little power play to flex his muscles. After this, things would be fine, Kyle thought. He hoped they'd get along like he did with Ochoa. But, before Kyle could make the friendly offer to trade mattresses, Leonard pulled Kyle's off the bunk and slid it on top of his own. The empty metal frame which remained would hold Kyle's weight, but he certainly wouldn't be able to lay on it comfortably. "I need one of those, Leonard," he said.

"Yeah, I hear that. But, I need two of 'em," Leonard answered, laying down on top of them in his bunk. When Leonard raised his arms to cradle his head, Kyle saw the Tiger tattoo on his bicep. It was the mark of the Tigres. Leonard might be new to the prison, but being a part of the Tigres meant he had more allies at Stevenson Youth than Kyle ever would.

"Hey man. Seriously, I'm going to need that mattress back," Kyle repeated.

Leonard looked totally relaxed. He was laying down with his eyes closed and his hands clasped behind his head. He didn't even respond to Kyle.

"Leonard," Kyle called out.

Finally, Leonard opened his eyes. "Shut the fuck up," he said. "If I hear you speak again, I'm gonna rip your tongue out of your mouth and eat it." With that, Leonard closed his eyes and went to sleep.

Kyle sat on the floor of his cell going through his newspaper clippings as Leonard took a long afternoon nap. Kyle's guilt about the crash always made sleep difficult to come by. And now, with a new cellmate that he couldn't trust, and no mattress on his bunk, Kyle wondered when he'd sleep peacefully again.

The folder of articles laid out in front of him helped to fill in some of the blanks and unclear spaces in Kyle's memory. This time around, all twelve of the kids, plus the driver of the bus, were still dead. His best friend Joe was, of course, dead, too. But this time, Kyle had been accused of first degree murder for having boarded up his own house, then killing Joe by banging his head into the floor.

Since 2016 Kyle boarded up the house, his own fingerprints were all over the boards and the nails, leaving 2014 Kyle without a leg to stand on when defending himself. He was also convicted of arson for trying to burn the house down. And, finally, he was convicted of thirteen counts of manslaughter for crashing into Bus #17 and sending it over Banditt Drawbridge as he ran away from the scene of his first crime.

Kyle wondered whether Radbourn was less friendly to him in this new timestream because he had a much more serious rap sheet now, and in this reality he'd caused the crash while running away from a murder.

He saw the silk blot sitting in his folder. Just as Allaire had said, going back in time had only made things worse. He was now serving a twenty-two year sentence, instead of eight. And after coming face to face with Radbourn's contempt for him, then meeting his new gangbanger cellmate, Kyle could only wonder what other surprises might be in store for him.

There needed to be a way to fix this. He considered the silk blot again, but going back had made things worse. He wondered, *what would be different this time?* Until he could answer that, going through the silk blot again didn't make sense. He had to try to work things out in this reality, otherwise who knew what might face him in another timestream?

He started to put his clippings back into his folder when everything in front of him started sliding back and forth on the floor. Then, he felt the ground swaying. Kyle grabbed hold of his bunk and instinctively brought one of his arms above his head to guard against anything that might fall. He heard the rumble of his foot locker sliding across the ground. The swaying continued for about ten seconds. Then, just after it stopped, the lights went out, leaving the room mostly dark, except for what little light came in through their tiny window.

"What the fuck?" Leonard asked, sitting up in his bunk. "A fuckin' earthquake? In New York?"

Kyle tried to look around the dark room for any damage. He could see that both bunks had shifted a little, and there was a big crack now near the ceiling on the wall opposite the door. He walked to the door of the cell and peeked out through the small glass window. "Looks like power's out in the whole cell block."

"Shut the fuck up, Kyle," Leonard snapped. "I'll tell you when it's time to speak." Leonard didn't bother getting up. He just lay in his bunk on both mattresses. "Earthquakes are some straight up West coast shit. They ain't supposed to happen here. You think they're gonna cancel visiting hours tomorrow 'cause of this?" Leonard asked. "My girl's supposed to come."

Kyle did not speak.

"I asked you a question, bitch," Leonard snapped.

"I—I don't know," Kyle stammered. "That was my first earthquake too."

Leonard turned to face the wall. "I hope that shit doesn't get cancelled."

"Hey, uh, Leonard?" Kyle said, turning toward him. "You think I could have my mattress back? It's gonna be real hard to sleep without one."

"Nah, man," Leonard answered. Kyle waited for more of an explanation, but nothing came.

"Listen, Leonard, you proved your point—" Kyle started.

Leonard sat up. "How the fuck do you know what my point is?"

"I just meant—"

"You want a new mattress," Leonard said. "Put in for a cell transfer. That's my point. Otherwise, get used to it."

As much as Leonard was proving a troublesome cellmate, Kyle had been in this cell since he'd been sentenced. This was also the cell where he'd found the two silk blots. He had no idea whether a silk blot could even be sent to another cell, and even though he had no intention right now of time weaving again, he wasn't about to transfer cells just because this gangbanger told him to.

"Leonard, we got off to a bad start," Kyle said. "How do we make this okay? You know the guards aren't gonna just let you keep both mattresses once they see that my bunk doesn't have one."

"That's why we're gonna put the mattress on your bunk during rounds, and I'll take it back when it's time to sleep," Leonard said. "Everybody wins."

CHAPTER 7

FEBRUARY 22 & 23, 2016

a few hours later

IT TOOK KYLE FOREVER TO FALL ASLEEP THAT evening. He wanted to wait until Leonard passed out, but after his nap, Leonard was content to just lay in his bed and rap hip-hop songs to himself. Kyle folded his pillow over his head and finally drifted off sometime after midnight, hoping the power would come back by morning. Maybe a visit from his girlfriend would make Leonard less of an asshole.

When Kyle woke up to the burning smell sometime a few hours later, he wasn't sure whether Leonard had poked him in the ribs, or if he'd just dreamt it. He saw the orange glow and popped into a sitting position to find that the cell was quickly filling up with smoke. His back felt sore and he groaned as he sat up.

There was a fire in the middle of the floor, where Kyle had sat just a few hours earlier. He knew right away that the papers burning were his clippings. Everything he'd saved from the day after the crash disintegrating before his eyes. Kyle quickly got up, threw on his slippers and started stomping out the fire. Most of the pile would be unsalvageable, though.

He looked at Leonard, who closed his eyes as soon as Kyle made eye contact. Kyle could feel the heat on his legs as he stifled the flames. "What the fuck, Leonard?"

Leonard pretended to act sleepy. "What's going on?"

"Would you stop?" Kyle said, stifling the last of the fire. "There's no one else here. You don't have to pretend you were sleeping. Why would you—?"

Kyle looked at the door. He heard the lock turn over and then saw the two flashlights.

"What the hell's going on in here?" Officer Manning asked. Manning looked like a surfer, but he had a temper as bad as any of the guards at Stevenson. Officer Staley—one of the longest tenured guards—followed him into the cell. They shined their lights on the charred remains of Kyle's clippings and then onto Kyle, standing right next to them.

One of them turned their light on Leonard, who played the whole sleepy routine again, this time even more convincingly.

"You starting a fire in here, Cash?" Manning asked. "You know matches are on the class A contraband list? If you'd set off the alarms, you'd be heading for the SHU right now." SHU was short for Solitary Holding Unit. It meant 23 hours a day by himself, and an hour walking around in a cage outside. No visitors. No books. No personal items. Nothing.

"I didn't start the fire," Kyle said. He wished he could be as convincing telling the truth as Leonard was when he was bullshitting. But, Kyle knew how the situation looked. "I don't have matches," he said meekly.

Staley walked over to Kyle's bunk. "Where's your mattress?"

Kyle looked at Leonard who quickly used his pinky to make a slashing motion over his throat, threatening Kyle. "He, uh, he took—"

"I hurt my back," Leonard said, "so he let me borrow his."

Staley didn't pay any attention to what Leonard said, because when he picked up Kyle's pillow, he found a cigarette lighter underneath. Staley tossed it to Manning. Kyle looked at Leonard in disbelief.

Manning walked over to Kyle and got very close to him. "Not good, Cash." Kyle could feel his breath on his face as Manning pulled his billy club from his belt. He stepped back and Kyle winced in anticipation of being hit. Kyle realized that Leonard must've stuck the lighter underneath his pillow before he poked him to wake him up.

Staley walked over to Manning and spoke to him quietly. "You know, Mikey, you put too much of a beatin' on the little pyro, you gotta do an incident report, explain it to the warden, all that . . . One big pain in the ass."

"I don't care—" Manning started.

"Warden's gonna care, Mikey," Staley said. "Mayor's watchin' him. You know he's gonna care."

"Sick pyro fuck," Manning responded, shaking his head and holstering his billy club."

Staley made eye contact with Kyle. "All of our systems are shut down with the power out. We'll deal with this in the morning. Any more issues in here, Cash, and your big trouble is gonna turn into unimaginably big trouble. Got it?"

"I gotta say," Leonard said. "I'm a little concerned with him stayin' in here with me. Who's to say he doesn't start another fire and burn the whole cell block down?"

Manning held up the lighter. "I got this now. You'll be fine. Go to sleep, inmates."

"And hey, Pitkin," Staley said. "None of your gang shit's gonna fly in here. Just ask your fellow Lions or Tigers or whatever the hell you're called." Kyle knew Staley was aware that the Tigres pretty much ran Stevenson Youth. The guards had to talk a big game, but when it came down to it, even they were afraid of getting too far on the bad side of the more powerful gangs. Everyone had cousins or friends on the outside.

Kyle wished he could defend himself, but he just watched the guards walk out of their cell. He cleaned up the burnt clippings from the floor and tossed them into the trash container. Scared as he felt to roll the dice with another trip through the time tunnel, living in this reality was quickly proving itself to be unsustainable.

Leonard just laid in his bunk with a self-satisfied look. Everything tangible Kyle had to remember the kids from the crash was gone now. Even his memory was tainted—a combination of recollections from the original crash, the second crash after his father had tried to stop it from happening, and this third version of the crash which Kyle caused while running from the police.

Kyle felt his stomach drop as he tossed the remains of his clippings and his folder into the garbage bin, and saw the stringy piece of burnt material underneath them. It was the silk blot, but it no longer looked sleek and other-worldly. Instead, it was just a blackened piece of fabric now. Kyle tried to poke his hand through, but he might as well have been trying to enter the time tunnel with a dish towel at that point.

Kyle had no question that he'd been better off before ever going through a silk blot. But now, his emergency exit from this horrid new timestream was destroyed just as he was coming to the conclusion he might really need it. He closed his eyes, despondent at the thought that his current reality was as good as life would ever get.

CHAPTER 8

KYLE EXPECTED TO BE SENT RIGHT TO SOLITARY as soon as the lights were back on, but he wasn't.

At breakfast in the chow hall, Franc, another one of the Tigres, walked up right behind him and just took his tray of food. "Take a hint, faggot, and put in for a transfer," Franc said. He took Kyle's tray over to his table, where Leonard and some other Tigres just glared at him, silently daring him to tell one of the guards.

Later that morning, Kyle tried to rest in the cell while Leonard was out at visiting hours. Just as he started to doze off, though, he heard the lock on the cell, and then the door opened. He figured his punishment for the night before had finally come.

Officer Radbourn walked in and Kyle didn't say anything. He didn't need to anger him again—not when punishment was already on the way.

"Inmate, I've got a . . . Sillow Cash here to see you. Home address is 1363 East Almond Boulevard, Jacksonville, Florida."

"I'll accept the visitor," Kyle said. He got up and followed Radbourn into the auditorium. He saw Leonard sitting with a girl who looked like she could be his sister. Short and bulky like him. Skin tatted up beyond recognition, and a scowl that said "fuck off."

Kyle scanned the room and found his father. "Thanks, Ol—Officer Radbourn."

Kyle had memories now of Sillow coming to visit him a lot during the past two years. If there had been one positive thing to come out of his traveling through time, it was that in this new reality, he'd spent time with his father and they'd gotten to know each other a little.

Kyle looked to make sure none of the guards were looking right at them, and then hugged Sillow tight. When he felt Sillow start to pull away, Kyle hugged him harder, choking back tears.

"You just got back," Sillow said.

"Yeah," Kyle answered. "Did you know?"

Sillow sat down, and wrinkled his brow. "Know what?"

"This whole time, these two years since the crash that you've been visiting me . . . Did you know that I'd go back and it wouldn't work?"

"I . . . I don't know, actually," Sillow said. "I don't remember knowing, but I know *now* that we tried to stop the crash two years ago together and it didn't work. I can't explain."

It hurt Kyle's head to think about. He wondered how Sillow could visit him for two years *after* the day they failed to stop the crash, but never say anything. Then again, this reality didn't exist until Kyle went back. If he couldn't explain it, he couldn't blame his father for not being able to either.

"It's really bad here right now, dad," Kyle said, his voice cracking. "Going back made my life go from bad to worse . . . I've got this new cellmate who's . . . I don't know."

"Who's what?" Sillow asked, looking sympathetically at his son.

"He's scary, dad," Kyle whispered, self-conscious that someone might hear. "I got twenty years to go, and . . . I don't . . . I don't know if I can do it." He quickly ducked around Sillow and sat in a seat where he was blocked from most of the other inmates. He bit the inside of his cheek to try to stop his tears, and prevent a full crying jag. The last thing Kyle needed was to look weaker right now. "I don't even think I can survive in here anymore. Without Ochoa . . . "

"What's the issue with this guy?" Sillow asked.

"He wants me to put in for a cell transfer," Kyle said.

Sillow shrugged. "Then do it, son—"

"You know how it works, dad," Kyle said. "I back down on this, then these guys *own* me. It's not like the outside . . . I need you to get me a silk blot."

"Last time I checked, they don't sell those at Wal-Mart," Sillow said.

"The woman who originally sent me back," Kyle said. "In *this* 2016, she hasn't come to see me. She thinks I'm a murderer. I need you to find her and tell her I need a silk blot . . . Myrna Rachnowitz. Tell her I'll get it right this time. Tell her if she gets me out of here, I promise I'll save her brother's life."

"Kyle," Sillow said. "Is that really something you can promise? What if you make it even worse? Seems like maybe there are forces at play," Sillow sighed, "I don't know, like, forces bigger than us."

Kyle wiped away a tear, hoping no one would see. "I have no choice, Dad. I can't do this. I really can't."

Sillow patted him on the back. They'd never spoken about it, but Kyle knew that Sillow had done time in his younger days. "Every inmate's said a million times 'I can't.' I promise, you'll get past this. You just gotta stand tall."

"Tell Myrna I need the silk blot soon," Kyle said. "These guys are going to do whatever they can to get me out of that cell, but I don't know if she can send a silk blot anywhere else in the prison. Promise me you'll go find her?"

"Sure, but I ain't makin' *her* any promises," Sillow said. "I made enough promises I couldn't keep to fill five lifetimes."

"Just try," Kyle said.

He wasn't as sure as Sillow that he could somehow tough it out and make everything okay. If Sillow couldn't come through and get another silk blot opened in Kyle's cell, Kyle would have no choice but to put in for a transfer. But until he was sure that getting out of this incredibly fucked up timestream wasn't a possibility, Kyle had no choice but to "stand tall" and try to survive.

CHAPTER 9

FEBRUARY 23, 2016

moments later

WHEN KYLE GOT BACK TO THE CELL, LEONARD was sitting on his bunk looking at the half-burnt remains of Kyle's clippings. He'd picked the ones from the garbage that still had some readable parts to them.

He considered voicing his disgust, but didn't. *What difference would it make?* he thought. Instead, he just avoided looking at Leonard and laid down on the hard metal of his bunk.

"Why'd you save old newspapers?" Leonard asked. "You like reading about those kids you killed, you sick fuck?"

"I'd rather not talk about it," Kyle said. He hated

feeling like he had to walk on eggshells in his own home. He'd gotten so used to feeling somewhat comfortable in prison, he'd forgotten sometimes that he owed it all to Ochoa.

Leonard pulled one of the articles close, trying to make sense of it despite the burns. "For a murderer, you sure are a pussy."

"Excuse me?" Kyle said.

"Excuuuuse me?" Leonard answered back, in a mocking, feminine tone. "You heard me, pussy."

Kyle had no choice but to let it go, just like he let it go that Leonard had burnt his stuff in the first place, or that now he was looking through it. Standing his ground was one thing, but he knew not to push it with a guy like Leonard.

"Real talk now, son," Leonard said, sitting up in his bunk. "I've been patient with you . . . All my boys in here have been patient with you. Now, it's time for you to put in for a transfer. My boy Raffy in Block D's gonna move in here, and you can go where's he's at now. He already put in the request. You do the same, and it'll get done."

"Why do you care so much?" Kyle answered.

Leonard hopped off his bunk to the floor in the middle of the cell. He looked in the air and took a deep breath as if he were dealing with a frustrating young child and he was trying to control his temper. "None of your fuckin' business . . . Just put in for the fuckin' transfer and you can do your time, and I'll do mine," he said slowly, ensuring that Kyle knew he wasn't asking.

Kyle sat up too. After starting the fire, he had no idea how far Leonard was capable of going.

When Leonard walked to the door and peeked out the small window, Kyle stood up. "Listen, Leonard, this has been my space for almost two years. Give me a few days."

"For what?" Leonard asked. "No, this isn't a fuckin' negotiation."

"Two days," Kyle said.

"No days," Leonard said.

Kyle could tell by the look in Leonard's eyes as he moved toward him that they were done talking. Leonard grabbed Kyle's right wrist and pulled it toward his face. The back of Kyle's hand made contact just below Leonard's eye. Leonard grabbed harder as Kyle tried to pull his hand away. Again, Leonard snapped Kyle's hand against his face. He was making Kyle hit him.

"Make a fist," Leonard said, still clutching his wrist.

"What? No!"

Leonard's eyes made him look insane. He twisted Kyle's wrist so hard it felt like it was going to break. "Make a fist, pussy."

Kyle clenched his hand into a fist. Without any hesitation, Leonard grabbed Kyle's wrist with his other hand and started head-butting his fist, over and over. Leonard smiled as he used Kyle's fist to punch himself in the face.

"What the hell are you doing, Leonard?" Kyle asked. But Leonard was in a zone. Every time he lifted his head before bashing his face against Kyle's hand, Kyle could see that he was laughing. Leonard didn't stop for a good minute—even as he opened up a cut on his left eyebrow. Each 'punch' hurt Kyle's hand more and more.

"You think anyone's going to believe I beat you up?" Kyle said. "This is stupid."

Suddenly, Leonard stopped. Kyle saw the blood dripping over his eye. Leonard blotted it with his finger, looked at it and smiled. "You're right."

The first punch to the side of his head felt to Kyle like he'd walked into a wall. After two more blows, Kyle was on the floor, curled on his side and protecting his head with his arms from any further beating. Leonard kicked him in the ribs for what felt like several minutes. Kyle kept shifting his body around as he writhed on the floor, trying to protect himself.

He rolled over and watched Leonard pound on the metal door of the cell. In less than a minute, Officers Gee and Forsyth came in. Leonard told them that Kyle had attacked him, and he'd hit Kyle trying to defend himself. For a guy who didn't sound like he had many brain cells in him, Leonard was a great liar, Kyle thought to himself. The little details came so easily to him.

As Kyle slowly stood up, he started to form the words to defend himself—disputing the story Leonard had put out there.

"Are you kidding me, Pitkin?" Gee asked him. "You're telling me *he* came at *you?* Not fucking likely." Kyle didn't like Gee, but he was an equal opportunity asshole and didn't play favorites.

"I swear," Leonard said, maybe not wanting to go too far out of his way to convince anyone he'd lost a fight.

"Whatever this shit is," Gee said. "Work it out."

"I don't feel safe with him in here," Leonard said, but it lacked the conviction he'd started with.

"It's prison," Gee said. "You're not supposed to feel safe."

Officer Forsyth moved closer to Kyle, and looked

at his eye. Forsyth looked more like an accoun-
tant than a prison guard, but he didn't take shit
and he went by the book, so most of the inmates
respected him. "I don't like the way this eye looks,
Gee," Forsyth said. "Warden would probably say
somethin' like this has gotta get looked at by the
infirmary."

"Alright," Gee said, sounding bored with the
whole thing already. "Take him down."

Forsyth gently pulled Kyle toward the door by
his upper arm.

"Seriously," Gee said. "I see something like this
with the two of you again, I'll throw you both in
SHU for a month. You'll be praying for the time
you can reunite in your unhappy little home."

Stevenson Youth's physician, Dr. Krebb, was only
in the building a day or two a week, which meant
there was always a long wait to see him. Since there

was only one exam room, the prison's nurse, Mrs. Waukegan, sat at a small desk next to the waiting area when the doctor was in with one of the inmates.

Kyle's head throbbed from being punched. He was happy at first for the excuse to get out of his cell, but he was on hour three now—with one inmate still ahead of him—of waiting for treatment that would likely consist of an icepack, and maybe a couple of Advil. He wished it were like a regular doctor's office and there were some magazines, or something—anything—to keep him occupied.

"He got you good!" the other guy waiting said to him. They'd never spoken before, but he was one of those guys that everyone knew. His name was Rakeem, and he was young, but he strutted around Stevenson like he owned the place. Kyle would've been shocked if he was even fifteen.

"I just fell," Kyle said.

Rakeem cocked an eyebrow at Kyle's answer. "Yeah, you fell alright," he said. "Fell into your new cellie's fist! You got fucked up, son. Ain't no shame in that."

"Whatever," Kyle said. "I don't really feel like talking."

"That's alright," Rakeem said, flashing a toothy smile. "I know everything you could tell me already anyway. I know everything that goes down 'round here."

"It's been a shitty day," Kyle said. "I just wanna get this over with."

"Good luck with tryin' to move this shit along," he said loudly enough for Nurse Waukegan to hear. Then, he lowered his voice, back to a normal speaking level. "You gotta be able to defend yourself better than that. Especially when you got a spot like yours. I wouldn't wanna give that up neither."

The kid was a natural charmer. Self-assured. The kind of guy who grows up to be a politician—if not for the criminal record. Kyle had no interest in talking right now, but wondered what he meant about not wanting to give up his cell.

"On the other hand, you can't blame the Tigres if they tryin' to fill that power vacuum, now that Kingpin done escaped," Rakeem said. "You're just like some, what do they call it? Collateral damage."

"Who's 'Kingpin?'" Kyle asked.

"You know, Coke-choa," Rakeem answered, laughing to himself. "E-choa. Meth-choa. He could *cho-a* you whatever you needed, as long as you *choa-ed* him the money."

Kyle couldn't believe what he was saying.

"Who are you talking about?" Kyle asked. "Ochoa wasn't dealing."

Rakeem gave him that get-the-hell-out-of-here look again. "Yeah, okay . . . "

"I'm serious," Kyle said.

Rakeem smiled to himself like he'd just heard something mind-blowingly ridiculous. "Oh shit! Either you was in on it, or you're the dumbest motherfucker in here. Cause your boy was dealin' to the whole prison, brah. You know this! Come on!"

Kyle tried to think about whether this version of Ochoa—the drug dealer Ochoa—was part of this messed up new reality he'd created, or whether he'd just been oblivious. Again, Kyle could feel himself going back in his mind to memories which conflicted with each other. He *did* remember an Ochoa who was different—more involved in the prison's social structure. A bit more threatening to Kyle. If he tried really hard, he could remember Ochoa packing up small lumps of hash into plastic wrap lifted from the chow hall. But he could also remember kind, goofy Ochoa, who kept to himself except to remind other inmates to give him and Kyle a wide enough berth to peacefully do their time.

He'd only gone back and forth through the time tunnel twice, and Kyle felt overwhelmed and confused by all of the different memories from different timestreams. No wonder Allaire seemed a bit crazy sometimes. Kyle couldn't imagine how many memories on top of each other she must be contending with.

"Yo, Nurse, seriously, how much longer?" Rakeem shouted, jarring Kyle out of the intense revelation that he *did* know the drug-dealing version of Ochoa who Rakeem had described.

"We'll call you when it's your turn, inmate," Nurse Waukegan answered in her monotone voice, then she went back to reading her book.

"Ochoa had the competitive advantage and ran with it," Rakeem said. "And now, the Tigres want their turn in the magic cell. But, yo, even if you get yourself killed, I respect you for tryin' to stand your ground."

Kyle scrunched up his face. "Magic cell?"

"C'mon. You knew! You had to know, brah!" Rakeem laughed again—the concept of Kyle's obliviousness too much to handle.

Kyle racked his brain. He tried to recall anything. This time, though, he came up empty. "Whatever, man. I'm dumb, I guess," Kyle said. "Enlighten me, would you?"

"That's why those bangers want your cell so bad, brah," Rakeem continued. "Coke-choa had a little hideaway spot—a little modification to the cell—that gave him that advantage over anyone else trying to keep their shit hidden from the guards. No one ever ratted him out, and in return, whenever anyone needed something to disappear for a minute, he'd stash it away. No questions asked."

"Where was this hiding place?" Kyle asked.

"No idea," Rakeem answered. "I'm sure your buddy Leonard knows, though."

"So he wants to move drugs through the cell," Kyle said.

"And you're not exactly Tigre material, if you don't mind my sayin'," Rakeem said. "But if he gets his homeboy in there, he can help guard the stash, hide it, sell it . . . Tigres take over the whole business."

The nurse stood up as another inmate exited the

doctor's office. "Rakeem Rodgers?" she called out, looking back and forth between Kyle and Rakeem, waiting for one of them to respond.

"Really?" Rakeem barked at her. "You think white-boy here is *Rakeem Rodgers*? C'mon lady!"

Kyle and Leonard didn't speak that evening until just before lights out when Leonard casually sat up in his bunk and told Kyle, "I just wanna let you know, it's officially time to watch your ass. It ain't just me anymore. You got a target on your back."

"Leonard," Kyle said. "I'll put in for a transfer. Just call off your boys."

Leonard shook his head. "Bad timing, son. You coulda had that deal before. Now that the whole prison knows the Tigres got an issue with you, we can't just squash this shit. We gotta send a message. Loud and clear . . . Anyway, good night,"

Leonard said, turning toward the wall and closing his eyes.

Kyle waited for nearly an hour until he was sure Leonard was asleep, before he closed his eyes. He woke up over and over, afraid he was going to be attacked in his sleep. *This was no way to live,* he thought. He needed to escape. He needed a silk blot.

CHAPTER 10

FEBRUARY 24, 2016

the next morning

KYLE USED THE BRUISES ON HIS FACE AS AN excuse to get him out of his daily activities, including meals and yard time. Although he had these memories now of the "Bad Ochoa," he wanted proof. If the secret stash spot Rakeem had mentioned was really there, it would be something tangible that linked these newer, less vivid memories with the ones that felt older, and more real, in Kyle's head.

As soon as Leonard headed out for breakfast, Kyle went to work going through the cell. He started on his own side and carefully felt along each cinderblock brick, and the space in between them, looking for something loose. He checked his own foot locker, and his desk, looking for something possibly hidden underneath. Finally, he moved his metal bunk to the center of the cell and examined the floor underneath. Nothing.

Kyle gave a peek through the small window on the cell door, and then quickly started the same examination of Leonard's side of the room. Kyle hoped that Sillow would be able to convince Myrna Rachnowitz to send him a silk blot, and that Kyle could get out of Stevenson Youth Correctional before Leonard and the Tigres got the chance to send their "message."

Kyle's desire to leave again through a silk blot wasn't based on the misplaced hope that a third time trying to stop the bus crash would actually be successful. It was simply a means of escaping his current situation. And at this point, any risk in going back, like running into 2014 Kyle and his head blowing up, felt more than worth it. Kyle couldn't possibly imagine returning next time to a timestream any worse than the one he currently inhabited.

He checked the bricks on Leonard's side of the room, his foot locker, and his desk. He didn't see anything out of the ordinary. When Kyle lifted the two mattresses up from Leonard's bunk, he finally did find something strange—two wooden rulers.

They were the kind you used in math class and they were just laying along one of the rails. Kyle noticed that the ends of each of them looked rough, like they been scraped against something over and over. He pulled Leonard's bunk to the middle of the cell now and checked out the floor underneath. Kyle still didn't see anything unusual. He held the rulers in his hands and went through the cell again, looking over all of the areas he'd looked at already.

Kyle scanned the room over and over again, turning like a kid trying to make himself dizzy. He looked at the ceiling, but there was nothing— not even a vent. *Am I crazy?* he wondered. For the first time, Kyle doubted even the things that had happened since he'd returned from 2014. He even wondered whether the conversation with Rakeem was a part of this timestream, a memory from another, or even something out of a dream.

After scanning for another few minutes, Kyle noticed a crack in the cement between two of the gray cinder block bricks that looked just slightly off. Perhaps it was from the earthquake the other day, he thought. But Kyle looked at the other bricks, trying to find more cracks, and couldn't.

He walked up to the crack, which was against the far wall of the cell on Leonard's side. He felt the cinderblock on top, trying to see if it moved at all, but it didn't. But when Kyle touched the block underneath the crack, he could feel it give a little. He bent down and saw now that there were cracks which ran all the way around the perimeter of this single brick.

Kyle tried pushing it, but it didn't go anywhere. He wondered if he could pull it out. The crack was too thin for his fingers, though. *How would anyone get their fingers in there?* he wondered. Then he realized. *The rulers.*

Kyle lifted up the mattresses on Leonard's bunk again and grabbed the two rulers. He slid one into the crack on one side of the brick, and one into the crack on the other side. He used each one to pry the brick, a few centimeters at a time, out from the wall.

Once enough of the brick was sticking out, Kyle used his hands to remove the whole thing. He was surprised at how much lighter it was than he thought it would be, but then he saw why. It was only half of a brick. From the front, you could never tell, but the back part of the brick was missing, which left a hidden space between the back of the brick and the wall.

Kyle laid the brick on the floor and bent down to look inside the hole. He saw a cigar box filling most of the empty space. The box was worn and looked like it'd been used for a long time. He pulled it out and opened the lid, but there was nothing in there.

Kyle sat down and leaned against the wall. In all of his compounded memories, stuck on top of each other like heavy slabs, he had no recollection of this stash space. He couldn't believe he could know Ochoa so well and, actually, not at all.

The door swung open and Kyle looked up startled. After his shocking discovery, he'd stopped working quickly. He still had the half-sized brick sitting on the ground next to him. His adrenaline kicked in and he stood straight up at attention.

Officer Radbourn's eyes registered a look of shock as they immediately went to the empty space in the wall, and then right to the brick laying at Kyle's feet.

CHAPTER 11

FEBRUARY 24, 2016

moments later

RADBOURN WALKED OVER AND PICKED IT UP. "What the hell?" he said. "Get to your side of the cell."

He tossed the brick onto Leonard's bunk, where it made a stifled thud, landing on top of the two thin mattresses. Radbourn pulled his flashlight from his belt and shined it into the hole. He pulled out the cigar box, looked inside and then tossed it on the ground.

He stuck his hand in and felt along the inside. "You got some kind of stash box here, eh?"

"No!" Kyle said. "You've got to believe me. I . . . I never saw that before today."

Radbourn picked up the rulers from off the ground. "Oh, you just happened to find it? Bullshit. You were in on it with Ochoa, and you're trying to run the business without him now that he's gone."

"No, I noticed the cracks," Kyle said. "I'm as surprised as you are."

"Get your shit packed," Radbourn said.

"Packed?" Kyle answered, standing up.

"I'm locking this cell down until we can fix that wall," Radbourn said. "We'll find you a new cell until this is settled. If you're dealing at this prison, I will take you down, Cash."

Kyle thought about his conversation with Rakeem. If the wall were fixed, Leonard and the Tigres wouldn't be able to utilize the same competitive advantage Ochoa had.

"But—" Kyle started.

"But, nothing, inmate," Radbourn cut him off.

"Officer Radbourn," Kyle said, "I had nothing to do with it."

"We'll see what the warden thinks," Radbourn

said. "Get your shit together. All of your shit. I don't want to have to ask you again."

Kyle grabbed a fresh change of clothes, his blanket and his burnt papers. He couldn't have imagined making matters with Leonard worse, but this actually had. And now, any silk blot sent Kyle's way would be left inside a cell he couldn't access.

Radbourn got on his walkie-talkie. "We got a situation. Third floor, block C, cell twenty-three. I need admin and facilities up here for an unsafe living condition."

CHAPTER 12

FEBRUARY 25, 2016

the next morning

KYLE'S TEMPORARY CELLMATE, A ONE-ARMED GUY who called himself "Sparky," was completely uninterested in Kyle's presence, which allowed him a much-needed night of rest. He actually woke up feeling great until he remembered that he had made enemies with the most powerful gang at Stevenson. He had no choice now but to hope for a silk blot—and that he could survive until one arrived. Assuming Myrna and Sillow could get one to him, how Kyle planned to get into his old cell to retrieve it was another matter altogether.

Kyle did his best to look invisible during breakfast. He angled himself so no one could come up from behind without him noticing, and kept looking over his shoulder. Not that he had much confidence there'd be anything he could do to stop it when Leonard and his cohorts came after him.

He still ate every meal in the same spot he used to share with Ochoa in his earliest prison memories. The two of them would always eat in those seats, sometimes joined by one or two other inmates, but usually by themselves. There was very little about prison that varied day-to-day and mealtime seating was no exception.

This morning, Kyle had no appetite and mostly just moved his eggs around on his plate. He was thankful that he had English class after breakfast. Classes helped to pass the time at Stevenson, even though as a former honor student, he was bored by most of the curriculum.

He looked at the clock hanging in the Stevenson chow hall and saw that he still had ten more minutes until class. When he noticed the hands on the clock start to rattle, Kyle looked down at his tray.

He saw his orange juice shifting back and forth in his glass, making little waves. Then a jolt sent his tray up off the table and crashing back down.

Kyle looked at the guards and saw how confused they looked. Then one of the guards reached for his bullhorn. "Get under the tables," he screamed. "Under the tables."

After the initial jolt, the swaying continued for a while. From under the table, Kyle saw breakfast trays falling to the ground, one after the other. *Another earthquake?* he thought. He heard a loud crash, turned, and peeked out to see that the huge, metal clock on the wall had fallen. The swaying gradually stopped, and Kyle looked around, trying to gauge for certain whether the quake was over.

The earthquake had led to a short, stunned silence, but once everyone came out from their places under the tables, the mess hall was a madhouse, most of the inmates hooting with relieved revelry.

"Stay where you are," the same guard called through his bullhorn. "There could be aftershocks."

Kyle had lived his entire life in New York and not experienced one earthquake, and now there had been two this week. Very strange, especially considering he'd just come back from traveling through time. Kyle wondered whether there was any link between the two.

He pulled himself up off the floor, between the bench and the table, sliding his breakfast tray back in front of him. But, as he did, he noticed something carved into the table:

KC: NO CLASS—2/25/16

It was his initials, and today's date, and it was etched in the same spot where he'd sat for every meal over the past two years. It hadn't been there before—he knew that.

He wondered why anyone would take the time to tell him he had no class by etching it into a table in the cafeteria. "Class" wasn't something many of the inmates at Stevenson Youth tended to care much about.

Then, it hit him. He realized the message was a lot simpler than that. Whoever had done this didn't want him going to his class today. They'd put it in the perfect spot to make sure he saw it. *Who had done this?* Kyle wondered. *And, why?*

When there were no aftershocks for the remainder of breakfast, the inmates were advised to proceed to their next scheduled activity. As Kyle exited the mess hall, he considered making the left turn and going to class. *Was the message from the Tigres to try to scare him? Who else would've done it?*

He turned in the direction of his English class and started walking. On his way, Hector, one of the Tigres, walked past him and give him a wink. Kyle's heart started to race a little faster. He looked around for guards and there weren't any nearby.

A few seconds later, Kyle saw Leonard and three other guys standing in the hallway he had to pass through on his way to his English class. Eventually, one of the guards might shoo them away, but probably not before Kyle reached them.

Kyle turned around and walked quickly in the other direction, hoping he could get to his cell before this passing period ended. Now, Hector stood in his way. He grabbed Kyle's arm to turn him around. "Wrong way, Kyle."

When he turned, he saw Leonard and the other guys walking down the long hallway toward them. Kyle still couldn't spot any guards.

Quickly, Kyle threw his shoulder into Hector, brushing past him and running toward his cell. He still had to get down two long corridors before he had any chance of getting inside his cell.

After a few seconds, he looked back and saw Leonard, the three guys he was standing with, and Hector, all running after him. Kyle kept a good lead on them as he turned down the first corridor. He wanted to yell for a guard, but during this time of day, inmates weren't allowed in their cells, so there might not be a guard stationed nearby.

Kyle looked back again as he came up on the next turn and saw that the Tigres were gaining on him. One of them was far ahead of the pack and Kyle worried that he wouldn't be able to get into his cell before he caught up.

He turned and shouldered himself through the double door leading to cell block C. He heard the Tigre right behind him burst through only a few seconds later. The door to his new cell would be unlocked at this time of day when most inmates were occupied with class, or other activities.

Oh shit! Kyle thought, as he realized—way too late—that he had no way to keep these guys out of his cell once he got there. Just like he couldn't unlock his own cell, he couldn't lock the door of the cell either—only the guards could. He made it and slid inside. With only a few seconds before the Tigres got there, he tried to think of how he could keep them out. He panicked. He was worse off here than he would've been if they'd confronted him in the hallway near his class.

Leonard and four other Tigres walked in together.

"We didn't even have to drag you into the supply closet," Leonard said. "You made it easy on us. I'm thinking maybe our conversation the other day didn't get my point across." The other four stood behind Leonard.

Kyle thought of his dad's advice to "stand tall" as Leonard walked up very close to him. He could smell Leonard's oniony breath. He felt a strange tension in his shoulder blade—anticipating that he was about to get hit.

Kyle made a fist instinctively.

"You messed up, Kyle. Real fuckin' bad," Leonard said.

"And you ain't got no cellie to protect you no more," one of the other Tigres, Rob, called out. He looked proud of himself until Leonard shot him a squinty look.

"Now, if we're gonna take over Ochoa's share of the, uh, prison economy, we're going to need to make sure people know they can't fuck with us," Leonard said.

Leonard held his hand above his shoulder without looking back. "Gimme it, Griddle."

One of the other Tigres, a tall guy named Griddle, whose face was half-covered by a huge burn, stepped forward and handed Leonard a candy bar wrapper. As Leonard pushed on the bottom of the wrapper, Kyle could see that there was a blade coming out the end of the wrapper, like the edge of a box cutter.

Kyle took a step back and put his hands in front of him. "Leonard. Don't do it. This is a huge mistake."

Leonard stepped toward him. "Take your medicine, pussy." Leonard swung the blade toward Kyle's neck, but Kyle managed to step backward, away from it. He was going to butt up against the wall pretty soon. The other four Tigres stepped closer as the action moved away from them in the cell.

Kyle put his fists up, ready to fight for his life. He was taller than Leonard, and had longer arms. He was also outnumbered five to one. "Get out of here, Leonard. I'm not fucking around."

"You think *we're* fuckin' around?" Leonard asked, smiling in amusement that Kyle had put his hands up. "Hit me, you little bitch. Come on, I dare you."

Kyle felt unsure of what to do. Maybe, if he survived this and could find a way back into his old cell, there would be a silk blot waiting for him. But, for now, this was Kyle's reality.

Leonard looked like it would take a tank to knock him over, and Kyle knew the Tigres would jump him even if he happened to land a perfect punch. *Stand tall.*

"Pussy, you ain't gonna hit me," Leonard said.

For so long, Kyle's guilt made him feel like he deserved to die young and alone. But, his recent time travel had complicated Kyle's feelings, and he felt more removed from his guilt now. He still went to sleep every night praying he'd wake up in some other life where he hadn't been responsible for ending twelve kids' lives too early. But somehow, just *trying* to fix everything had reminded Kyle what hope felt like. And now, standing here in this untenable position—his life in the hands of a sociopath, and four other teenage convicts—Kyle was not inclined to just lie down and pay the ultimate price.

"You know what?" Kyle said. "Fuck you." He brought back his right fist as if he were winding up to land a haymaker, but instead delivered a fast left jab to Leonard's face, immediately bloodying his nose.

Leonard barely moved when Kyle's fist landed cleanly. Leonard pulled Kyle in by his shirt now, and put him in a chokehold. It was loose enough, at first, for Kyle to breathe regularly.

A few seconds later, Leonard firmed up his grip a bit and brought his blade up to Kyle's eye. "Should I carve up your face? Take out an eye?

Will that be a good reminder to everyone who sees you to not fuck with the Tigres? Or should I just fuckin' kill you?"

Kyle tried to shake Leonard off of him, but he couldn't get his arm to budge. Kyle felt himself becoming more and more light-headed. *This is how I'm going to die*, Kyle thought with only some of the bravery he'd felt moments earlier. *This is it.*

At first, Griddle didn't think there was a chance Leonard would actually kill the kid. But, the longer he choked him out, the more he thought he might.

He got an uneasy feeling just standing and watching. Griddle turned back and peeked out the door of the cell to make sure no one was coming.

No good was gonna come out of some kid dying in here. Griddle had been in the system long enough to know the way it worked—things got lax for a while and everyone could breathe a bit. But then something big happened, like a murder, and it took a long time to get back to the chill way of life. Ochoa escaping had already stressed the guards. This would put 'em over the edge, and make life for him, and all the Tigres, harder.

"Hey," Griddle called over to Leonard. "Let's get outta here before we get busted."

Griddle watched as each of the other boys looked to Leonard for a response. Griddle could tell that they wanted to go too. But, Leonard just kept squeezing Kyle's neck. By now, his eyes were starting to roll back in his head.

"Don't kill him, Len," Shawn called out.

"I'm just putting him to sleep," Leonard answered, out of breath.

"Wha', like in wrestling?" Shawn asked.

"Yeah," Leonard said. "Sleeper hold."

Kyle's last grasp on consciousness was fading when he felt a warm liquid splatter on his face. Suddenly, Leonard was off of his neck, and Kyle was on all fours catching his breath. He saw that the liquid on his arm was blood.

Kyle looked up and saw Allaire holding one of the Tigres by his hair as blood poured from his throat. She let him drop face first to the ground as another Tigre tried to grab her arms, while Hector threw a punch at her face. She ducked and jabbed her combat knife into Hector's belly, pulling it out quickly and turning toward Leonard and his two gangmates. She handled the knife like a ninja.

Kyle stood up as he caught his breath again and watched as Allaire swung her blade once at Raffy's face—he was their gangleader. She swung again, and this time, he barely got out of the way. Then in one fluid move, she turned and pulled him closer by the shirt, sliding the blade across his throat.

Leonard ran at her now with his blade and tried to stab her in the side. It was almost as if she had eyes in the back of her head, though. She swung Raffy's quickly dying body around toward Leonard and used Raffy like a shield. Then she pushed Raffy toward Leonard and both fell in a heap to the ground.

"What are you doing here?" Kyle asked Allaire. She shot him a look, but didn't say anything.

She moved toward Griddle now, and pulled her combat knife back to strike.

"Allaire, no!" Kyle yelled to her, springing to his feet. "I'm safe. You don't need to kill him. Let's get into your silk blot and get out of here."

Suddenly, Kyle heard a shredding sound. Allaire winced and an instant later her leg buckled. Kyle looked down and saw Leonard holding his make-shift boxcutter.

From the floor, Leonard grabbed hold of her other leg now, and he quickly dove on top of her, holding her wrists against the floor so she couldn't strike with her combat knife. She tried kicking him off of her, but he used his body weight to hold her down.

Kyle tried to pull Leonard off, but Griddle grabbed Kyle and pulled him backward.

Leonard still held one of Allaire's wrists and held his blade up to her face with his other hand. He smiled, enjoying the advantage.

Kyle turned to Griddle and hit him with a huge uppercut, dropping him to a knee. Then, he hit him once more in the side of the head, knocking him woozily to the ground.

He turned back toward where Leonard was straddling Allaire now. Kyle pulled his fist back and delivered a crushing punch to the side of Leonard's head, knocking him off of Allaire and down to the hard concrete floor of the cell. Allaire squeezed out from underneath Leonard and stood up.

Allaire stepped on Leonard's wrist, digging her foot into him as hard as she could.

Leonard winced and let his knife drop to the floor.

Kyle picked up the knife. "Let's go."

But now Allaire was straddling Leonard, her knife against his throat. "No!" Kyle screamed.

"Kill me. I don't fucking care," Leonard said to Allaire.

"Please, Allaire," Kyle said. "We don't need to."

Kyle gently lifted her off of Leonard by her armpits. Her eyes looked different than he'd ever seen them. Focused in a way he'd rarely seen anyone look.

"You okay?" Allaire asked.

"I think," he answered, looking around the carnage. "You?"

There was a commotion in the hall outside the cell. Voices were coming their way.

Allaire pulled a silk blot from the inside pocket of her jacket. "Come on. We need to get out of here."

CHAPTER 13

"HOW DID YOU KNOW I NEEDED YOU?" KYLE asked as he followed Allaire through the time tunnel. He was trying to piece together everything that had just happened. "You came back to save me, didn't you?"

"Kyle . . . " Allaire said, "*why* doesn't matter."

He was lining everything up in his head just as the words came out of his mouth. "You knew something bad was going to happen when those gangbangers cornered me and you came back to do something about it. That's why you left the message on the table. But the message must not have worked."

"Can we please stop talking about it?" she asked, continuing to move through the tunnel. "Please." He heard her voice crack.

"But what about your whole speech at the bus station? About how it's impossible to change the past?" Kyle asked. "If they were going to kill me—."

"They weren't going to kill you," she snapped, stopping and turning back to him. She shook her head, disappointed. "Can we please . . . ? I just completely broke every rule, every freaking principle I've known since I got dragged into this life in the first place. I'm out of answers now, Kyle! So, how about being part of the solution? Help me do my job instead of shining a light on how much I've messed up."

She started crying. Kyle pulled her into a hug and she collapsed in a ball in his lap. The hard ridged metal of one of the time tunnel's rungs poked him in the back.

"I did all of this because I'm in love with you," Allaire said "But, you? You're in love with some fairy tale idea that you can just go back and erase your big screw-up. Time travel therapy doesn't exist, Kyle. And if you could see that . . . If you could only see that . . . "

"I don't understand what you've done that's so wrong," Kyle said, still holding her.

She heaved her body as she cried. "You can *never* go back to your own time again to live," she said. "That's how bad I fucked things up . . . Those earthquakes were the universe reacting."

"I understand," Kyle said.

"Do you?" she asked, sitting up and putting her hands on his cheeks. "I'm serious. No more do-overs," she said. "The bus crash happens. End of story. Promise me you understand that."

Kyle nodded. He didn't *really* understand—how could he?—but he understood how serious she was. And he knew that nothing he'd done by going back to the day of the crash had amounted to anything but trouble.

She started moving again. "We need to get as

far away from here as we can," she said stoically. "You'll be a fugitive for as long as anyone believes you might still be alive."

They'd been climbing quietly through the tunnel for a while. As opposed to their usual flirty banter, this was a funereal atmosphere, with Kyle left mostly to thinking about Allaire's words earlier. They passed the rung for the year 2022, the year Kyle would've been released from his original prison sentence.

"Allaire, I know I can't go back now, but my life is *here*. We're literally passing it by," Kyle said. "It may not be much of a life, but tell me I can go back to it eventually."

Allaire moved close to Kyle's face. "You really *don't* get it, do you? If you think all you're cut out for is to be a convict, go on back. Back to your cell. Back to thinking about those kids—who you can't save anyway—twenty-four hours a day."

"I didn't say I wanted that," Kyle said. "Why do you care about me so much? I killed twelve kids. I deserve everything that came after. I deserve to be in that prison."

"You just rotting in a cell for one single mistake," she said. "That's something I couldn't stomach. I've been doing this a long time, and you're the only person I've ever broken the rules for."

Kyle stopped climbing and thought to himself for a moment. For the first time, he saw Allaire as part of something bigger. Everything he knew of her was in relation to him and the crash, but she had a purpose too. She had some type of job. But who she was working for, and why, remained a mystery. There were clearly rules, though, which meant that somebody was probably in charge. He wanted to know more about her—and more about how it all worked. If he went back now, he'd never know any of these answers. If he didn't, though, he'd be a man without a time. His life might begin to resemble Allaire's, for all the little he knew about it.

"Why break the rules for me, though?" Kyle asked.

She looked him in the eyes, as if she were still trying to answer the question herself. "There's something about you, Kyle. It's more than just how much I care about you. I . . . I just have a feeling."

"Okay," he said nodding. "Let's go."

Allaire smiled and started down the tunnel again. "I'm bringing you home."

"Where's home?" Kyle said.

"Wrong question," Allaire answered, the playfulness back in her voice.

"*When?*" Kyle asked, playing along dutifully. "*When* is your home?"

"There you go," she said. "Come on, just follow me." With that, she was off again, climbing through the tunnel toward an unknown destination in the future.

CHAPTER 14

THE FIRST THING KYLE DID WHEN HE EXITED the silk blot at the slot labeled 2060 was to spin around, and take in his first glimpse of the future. They were on the top of a building, and he noticed that it was pitch black. Even with just the moonlight, though, Kyle could tell from the buildings that they were still in New York City.

Less than a minute after they arrived, Kyle felt something tug on the back of his shirt. He stumbled backward until the back of his legs hit against something hard. He turned around and Allaire gently pushed him into a vehicle. Kyle sat in a soft leather seat, and watched as Allaire climbed into the vehicle after him, and then the doors slid shut. The flying vehicle had been completely silent as it landed behind them, and it was quiet now as it took off into the air.

Kyle tried looking out the window to see where they were going, but the bright orange tinting, combined with the lack of lights, made it hard to see.

Allaire pulled two straps from over each shoulder and crossed them like an X in front of her. "Buckle up."

Kyle secured the straps, then craned his head for a better look at the vehicle's driver, a hulking blond with solid shoulders. Even though he was sitting down, Kyle could tell he was built like a truck. "Where's he taking us?" Kyle asked Allaire.

"Just relax. We're in good hands," Allaire answered. "You could have a maniac flying this thing, and it'd still be less dangerous than trying to survive out there these days."

"Who says I'm not a maniac?" the driver asked

without turning around. He had an Australian accent.

Kyle felt the vehicle accelerate, and he could tell that they were ascending quickly into the air. He watched as Allaire placed her silk blot into a small glove compartment on the back of the seat in front of her.

The vehicle was long and thin, and when Kyle turned and looked backwards, he saw scalloped metal walls that made it look like the machine had a tail. As they leveled off and accelerated, the tail swung back and forth with every turn.

"What is this thing?" Kyle asked.

"We call it a 'pillar,' like caterpillar," the pilot said, reaching his hand behind him to shake Kyle's hand, while keeping the other on the H-shaped steering device. "Everett."

Kyle leaned forward and met his firm grip. "I'm Kyle."

"I know your name," Everett said. "My wife told me you were the first boy she ever fancied."

"Your wife?" Kyle asked. He looked over at Allaire, who just stared forward biting her lip.

"Yeah," Everett answered, sucking the air out of the vehicle. "My wife."

The Aussie turned and gave a quick glare at Allaire. He didn't look happy at all. For the first time, Kyle could see his eyes, blue and intense.

No one spoke for the rest of the ride, except once, a few minutes later when Kyle finally managed to catch Allaire's glance. "It's complicated," she whispered.

Everett spent more time tinkering with a touchscreen above his head than actually steering. Kyle noticed that the pillar had four little red fire alarm boxes on its ceiling, each covered with plastic, with small metal hammers mounted next to them. They looked like fire alarms, but were placed only inches from each other. If they were alarms, there'd be no need for four so close together.

A few minutes later, Kyle felt the pillar slow up and gently land. Everett pressed a few more buttons on the control panel, took out a huge key from the ignition, which looked like a tuning fork, and Allaire undid her seatbelts. "Welcome to the silo," she said.

Kyle followed the two of them out of the pillar, which from the outside looked like something out of the *Transformers* movies. He hopped down about three feet to the ground, and looking up, he saw that they were inside a tall structure, like a tower. The name "silo" made sense—the ceiling was at least a hundred feet above them, and the walls were rounded. Allaire and Everett spoke quietly to each other a few feet away.

There was a long staircase running in a spiral along the outer wall of the building. The stairs led from one loft to the next. Every room was built on top of a platform jutting out from the wall. Each platform was at a different height. Some of the rooms had bamboo dressing screens in place of the absent walls. Kyle assumed these were bedrooms. Others were completely open. The ground floor was part kitchen and part garage, with the pillar only about twenty feet from the refrigerator. Kyle could see into the first platform up, and it looked like some sort of surveillance or security area, with a bay of screens and computers lined up next to each other.

Allaire and Everett shared a short hug, but it didn't look to Kyle like a romantic one. Everett grabbed her tight, but the way she tapped his back looked more maternal than wifely. This was a relief to Kyle, who hadn't ever been made to feel jealous before when it came to Allaire.

Kyle followed Everett with his eyes as the large man walked up the spiral staircase to the room with all of the TV screens. Suddenly, he turned back down the stairs as if he'd forgotten something.

The building was unlike anything Kyle had ever seen. His head was spinning. It was too dark for him to get much of a look at 2060 New York City in the minute he'd spent out in the world before the pillar picked them up, but this building was unlike anything he'd ever seen in his life.

Everett opened a small hatch on the wall and grabbed something that looked like a first aid kit. He opened the box, pulled out an item that looked like a Q-tip, and walked toward Kyle.

"Open your mouth," Everett said.

Kyle considered asking why, but he was too overwhelmed with everything he was seeing. He didn't have the mental bandwidth to resist.

Everett swabbed the inside of his cheek, then turned away. "Thanks," he said, holding the Q-tip up as he walked back upstairs. Kyle expected some kind of explanation, but none came.

As soon as Everett went upstairs, Allaire turned away from the kitchen area and walked over to Kyle.

"When can I go outside to see everything?" Kyle asked. As baffled as he was about Everett and Allaire, and where that left Kyle's relationship with her, he was astonished and energized at the idea that he was actually in the future.

Allaire walked over to Kyle. "It's not safe out there."

Allaire grabbed Kyle's shirt and gently pulled him around to the other side of the pillar, pressing him up against the warm metal. She looked upstairs, to make sure Everett couldn't see them, Kyle assumed. "I wish we could spend the night together," she said, and then she kissed him fast and hard.

Kyle kissed her back at first, but then pushed her shoulders away. "But, instead, you'll be spending it with your husband. This is really strange, Allaire."

"It's not like that," she said. "At least for me it's not, I promise. Can we kiss now, and I'll explain another time?" she said.

Kyle thought about it, and then pulled her toward him.

A few minutes later, she grabbed his hand and

led him back into the center of the room. "Who else lives here?" Kyle asked, looking up and taking it all in again. There were twelve platforms, and four had bamboo privacy screens.

"At the moment, it's just Everett and I. But it's always evolving," she answered. "Neither of us would be here if it was safe to live in our natural timestreams."

"Your natural timestream?" Kyle asked. He saw Everett looking down at them, leaning on a metal railing lining the outside of the platform above them.

"It's as simple as it sounds," she answered. "It's the timestream you were born into. Ev and I don't get that luxury."

"Why here?" Kyle answered. "Why 2060?"

"This is the end of the line, Kyle," she said. "Or at least, the end of the time tunnel. We've never stayed here for long enough to see 2061 because neither of us has any idea what happens *after* 2060. Or if the world even exists."

Kyle looked around. "I'm totally confused."

"We never stay here longer than a day or two at a time," she answered.

"Where else do you go?" Kyle asked.

"Wherever I'm needed," she answered.

Kyle looked at her and saw how sad it made her to talk about all of this. "Why do you do it?"

Allaire looked away from him. "Because there's someone who won't stop until he wins . . . "

"Who's out there?" Kyle asked. "Who's trying to change the past?"

"An old friend," Allaire answered. "Listen, no more questions. You need to get some rest. I know I owe you more answers. Just remember, Kyle Cash, there's no turning back now. We have all the time in the world—literally—to get you up to speed."

Kyle almost felt dizzy trying to rationally consider the fact that he was in the year 2060. Somewhere, beyond this strange, tall structure, he was sixty-two years old. *If* he was still alive. "This is too much."

"I know, my . . . Kyle," she answered, putting

a hand on his shoulder from behind. "This isn't a job for people with any connection to a particular time or place. Ev's got nothing out there. This is it for him."

"What about you?" Kyle asked.

Allaire paused before answering. "I lost my connection the first time you left me in 1998," she answered. "And then . . . "

Everett was now leaning over the railing from upstairs and cut into their conversation. "Allaire, get up here! Quick!" he yelled down.

Allaire walked toward the staircase.

Kyle just watched her go, trying to respect that she wasn't ready to share everything with him yet. She stopped at the bottom of the stairs, though, and turned. "Come on."

"Really?" Kyle asked.

"Really. The best way for me to explain everything is for you to just *be* with me. I'll do my best to explain as we go. Okay?"

Kyle sighed, half-pleased and half-frustrated.

"Sure," he said, as he followed her upstairs to join Everett.

The platform was bigger than it looked from the main floor. They had a bay of six circular monitors playing static footage of different entranceways. Kyle assumed these were feeds from security cameras. The resolution was better than anything Kyle had ever seen on a screen. The picture looked so clear that Kyle was tempted to reach out and touch it.

On the other side of the room there was an Apple computer which didn't look very different than the one Joe Stropoli used to have in his family room. The huge monitor was covered up by a white blanket. Next to the mouse, hooked up to the computer was a device with ten small holes in it. All of them were empty except one which had a Q-tip inside of it. Kyle figured this was the same one Everett had swabbed in his mouth.

"What's up with the blanket over the screen?" Allaire asked.

Everett nervously tapped his desk with the key to the pillar. He looked at Kyle. "Should he be up here?"

"He knows so much already, Ev," she said.

"And that Q-tip has my spit on it," Kyle added, trying to sound firm, but realizing how silly it must've sounded before the words were even out of his mouth.

"He's not going anywhere, Ev," Allaire said. "We've gotta trust him."

Everett shook his head and looked troubled. "I wish I knew how to say 'no' to you, darling."

"Let's hope you never figure it out," she said with a soft smile. Kyle wanted to throw up in his mouth. This guy was either a complete cheeseball, or trying to rub Kyle's nose in the fact that he and Allaire were married. Or both.

"So, I did the D-track on him, but something weird happened," Everett said to Allaire.

"Am I allowed to ask what a D-track is?" Kyle

asked. Being in this room made him feel like he was in a futuristic sci-fi movie.

"We're gonna be here all night if all the kid does is ask questions," Everett said.

Allaire rolled her eyes and smiled at Kyle. "It's short for DNA Target Tracking. Anyone who travels through time needs to make sure they avoid seeing themselves in person. That goes for us too." She sat down on a rolling stool next to the computer. "By inputting our DNA into this machine, we can use something called astro-visual tracking to make sure the 2060 versions of ourselves are nowhere nearby."

"So you took that saliva from my cheek so you could see where I am in 2060?" Kyle asked excitedly.

"It's actually skin cells from your cheek, but whatever," Everett said, pulling the sheet from the monitor. The camera footage was clear, but Kyle didn't see himself. He just saw an empty kitchen—a bit more futuristic, but resembling a kitchen enough that Kyle knew what it was.

"This is a feed from inside of a building in California," Everett continued. "Near Los Angeles. It looks cushier than most things do in this fucked up world."

"You think he's in one of the West coast salvation units?" Allaire asked.

"Likely," Everett answered. "Or else LA's been having quite a laugh during everyone else's apocalypse."

Kyle looked at the screen and couldn't help but smile. A figure walked into the picture and he could tell immediately that it was him. Like looking in a mirror. What an amazing thing, he thought, to see himself in 2060!

The Kyle on the screen looked like he was alone, and started making a sandwich. The screen said it was four o'clock in New York, so it was lunchtime on the West coast.

Allaire took one look at the monitor and was

stunned. She put her hand up. "Wait, Ev, I—I just—I don't get it. It doesn't make sense."

"No, it does not," Everett answered. "Not at all."

"What doesn't make sense?" Kyle asked. "There I am."

"It's 2060, Kyle." Allaire said.

"Right?" Kyle answered. He looked at the image again. There wasn't a whole lot to notice. There was the kitchen, the sandwich on the counter, and himself. Clear as day. He was glad that he was so far away so he didn't have to worry about his head blowing up. *Wasn't that the whole point of the test?* he wondered.

Everett and Allaire looked at each other, then at Kyle, then back to each other. They looked confused, and a bit scared.

"What the fuck is going on?" Kyle said. "Would somebody just talk to me?"

"You look exactly the same," Allaire said. "Don't you see? You haven't aged."

At first, it didn't sound like a big deal to Kyle.

"Well, maybe I never go back and that's why I'm the same age. Maybe I just stay here."

"But, we can't take video of the future," Everett said. "This image is what you're doing *right now*. In 2060."

"The Kyle that's standing here right now next to me," Allaire said, "is forty-four years younger than the Kyle on the screen. *That Kyle* should look like an older man."

"This doesn't make sense," Kyle said. "Maybe you didn't do the swab right, or—"

"Easy there, tiger," Everett said. "Leave this to the professionals."

"Why hasn't he aged?" Allaire asked. "It makes no sense."

Kyle considered the magnitude of all of this. When he'd gone through the silk blot the first time, he hadn't bothered to wonder how many other people knew about time travel. Even right up until he and Allaire exited her silk blot in 2060, Kyle felt like the entire concept of time travel was small and personal—*his* journey to fix what went wrong on the morning of the bus crash. So far, his unsuccessful journey.

Now it was clear that he was a just small part of something much bigger. He just wasn't sure where he fit into it all yet, and clearly, neither were Everett and Allaire.

"Something's broken," Allaire said. "It must be. Are you sure this is a current image?"

Everett nodded, his eyes glazing over as he stared at the screen. "I don't know what to tell you. I'm at a loss." Then he paused and looked straight up at Allaire, "Is there any way he could be a Sere?"

"What's a Sere?" Kyle asked. But neither of them even looked his way.

"Get me a needle," Allaire said, pulling her eyes away from the screen for a second. "The only thing that explains this is if you're somehow getting an old feed."

Everett stood up, barely able to pry his eyes away from the screen as he backed away. He opened a closet built into the wall and pulled out a small suitcase. He opened it and rummaged through, before pulling out a small, clear plastic container. He handed it to Allaire and then sat down at the computer screen.

Everett held his face with his hands and watched, as if Kyle making a sandwich in California might reveal the answers to the greatest mysteries of the universe.

Allaire opened a small, travel-size sewing kit and started wrapping a spool of thread around a needle over and over, leaving the sharp tip exposed. Kyle's attention was split between watching Allaire work—cool and efficient, like she was in his cell earlier—and watching himself on screen.

"Kyle, honey, you ever get a tattoo?" she asked.

"No," he answered. He didn't like the way Allaire acted when Everett was around, and he really didn't like that she hadn't told him she was married. She was talking to him like he was her nephew or something. Perhaps she never envisioned bringing Kyle to 2060, but still . . .

Allaire walked up to the monitor, just as 2060 Kyle walked out of the picture for a minute, leaving his sandwich on the table. "I'm gonna mark the back of his neck, just below the shirt line," Allaire said to Everett, who nodded, still unable to break his eyes away.

"I'm going to have to give you a small tattoo right here," she said, touching the back of his neck in a way that made Kyle's entire back twinge.

"Why?" he asked.

"Just hold still," she answered.

Allaire worked quickly and Kyle grimaced through it, trying not to yelp as she pricked the back of his neck repeatedly. In a few minutes it was over and she tossed the homemade tattoo needle onto the desk in front of the bank of security monitors. She turned back to the screen and looked at the time stamp in the corner.

She used two compact mirrors to show Kyle the

uneven circle now permanently affixed to the back of his neck in blue ink.

The three of them sat with their eyes glued to the monitor, watching Kyle eat his sandwich.

"I need to talk to you when you have a moment," Everett whispered to Allaire, but loudly enough so Kyle could hear. "Alone."

"One second, Ev," she said. "Watch."

They sat waiting, as Everett tapped the pillar key nervously on the desk.

They watched as Kyle on the screen got up and brought his dish over to the sink. When he turned his back to the camera—probably located on a satellite miles above his apartment—it was clear as day. There, on the back of *that* Kyle's neck, was the same tattoo Allaire had just put on *this* Kyle's.

"I just don't understand it," Everett said, slamming his hands down on each side of the keyboard as he got up. Allaire stood up right after him, and they headed out of the room. "The only other person like this is Ayers."

"We'll be right back, Kyle," Allaire said, cutting him off. Kyle watched them head up the stairs and around the perimeter of the silo to a room three levels up.

Kyle wondered who Ayers was. Perhaps he was in charge, Kyle thought. Whoever he was, they shared something. Kyle just wasn't sure what that something was. And neither did Everett or Allaire. In any case, with each passing moment, Kyle was more certain that he didn't belong here. At least not yet.

He kept coming back to his conversation with Allaire on the bus. She said her job was to fix things that went wrong when people time weaved. Well, if she could fix things, why couldn't *he* fix the bus crash? So what if the universe didn't want him to? Thirteen lives were at stake for crying out loud, and Kyle felt a renewed sense that maybe he could take everything he'd learned from going back twice already and actually stop the crash from happening now. The more he thought about it, the more he was sure that he *could* fix things this time. Allaire said it was impossible, but he just saw that she didn't have all of the answers.

If he could stop the crash, he could go live in 2016 without being in prison. And without being responsible for twelve kids being killed. His last try had failed, and the terrible result had made him lose focus. Now that he had been to 2060, and seen a little bit about how it all works, he felt ready.

I don't want to be the person who gives up, he thought to himself.

He looked over the railing, down at the pillar only a few feet below. Then, he looked up at Everett and Allaire, three platforms up above him. He could see them look down at him from time to time. It was obvious they were talking about him. He was curious about what they'd all seen on the screen, but didn't trust that they'd share the whole story with him.

Kyle got up and walked to the screen, staring at

himself. It was him, no question. He was sitting at a table now, reading a book. Kyle wondered what his years between now and then held, and what, if anything, he could do to change those years, for better or worse.

Deep inside of him, Kyle felt that if he stayed here, he would never end up there, at that table, looking like a free man. He had no idea when Everett and Allaire would let him leave, especially in light of this new development.

He saw the key to the pillar sitting on the desk and remembered that Allaire had left a silk blot inside of the glove compartment. He grabbed the key, ran down the spiral staircase and hustled for the vehicle. He had absolutely no idea what he was doing.

CHAPTER 15

JULY 22, 2060

moments later

THE SLIDING DOOR TO THE PILLAR OPENED EASILY when he pulled the handle. Everett and Allaire were already bounding down the stairs toward him.

Kyle walked toward the glove compartment where Allaire had left her silk blot, then stopped and took a seat in the pilot's console, jamming the key into the same spot where he'd seen it before. If he couldn't close the door on the pillar, there was no way he was going to be able to get into the silk blot before they could stop him.

He searched the control panel for a button to close the door, but there were at least a hundred gauges and buttons on the console in front of him.

He found controls for the "Magnidrive Optical Input" and the "Vertical Calibration Stabilizer," but didn't see anything just labeled "doors." The screen above him came down and he saw a huge, electronic map of New York City.

As the pillar's engine began to roar, the side door of the silo flipped open. Kyle tested the controls and was able to point the nose of the pillar using the steering tool in front of him. He felt the vehicle rise and he was hovering now a few feet off the ground, powered by strong downward jets.

"Kyle! No!" Allaire screamed out. Kyle could only see her head through the open door. She looked panicked. "We need your help! Please, just power it down."

"Who's Ayers?" Kyle yelled back.

"He's the one we need to find," she yelled. "We need to stop him."

"Why?" he answered.

"I'll tell you everything I know," she yelled. "I promise."

"I need to help those kids," he yelled back. He wanted to jump right into the silk blot, but every time he took his hands off the steering device, the pillar started to float slowly toward the ground. He didn't know the controls well enough to keep it hovering while he grabbed the silk blot.

"Those kids are supposed to die, Kyle," she screamed. "That's just the way it is. Please come out here and just talk to us."

Kyle looked away from her when he shouted, "I just don't see it that way. I can't see it that way." Then he glanced down at his armrest and saw a button with a tiny picture of a lock on it. He pressed it and the side door to the pillar slid shut. Allaire had saved him from the Tigres. She deserved better than this betrayal, but he owed even more to the twelve kids on the bus.

He pulled back on the steering device and the pillar lurched forward out of the silo and up into the air, knocking the back of Kyle's head against the seat. He winced, his neck still very sore from the impromptu tattoo session. The pillar shot up quickly, rising above Everett and Allaire's silo. When he pushed in on the steering tool, the pillar slowed down and Kyle leveled out. It was nighttime, and from up in the air, Kyle could already tell it was a different world. The City that Never Sleeps was almost completely dark, and Kyle couldn't spot a soul. It looked like every other building was gutted and partially collapsed. Everything he could see down below was thanks to the glow of the moon.

The pillar hung in the air as Kyle cruised around, bobbing up and down a little bit with the wind. He pressed on the touchscreen map above his head and was able to set the autopilot to the next-to-last address in the history tab: Two twenty-five West Thirty-fifth Street. The pillar smoothly descended a few feet, turned and cruised ahead on its own.

As he let the autopilot fly him through the night sky, Kyle wondered whether he was in a one-of-a-kind vehicle, or whether seeing pillars flying through the sky was commonplace in the future, at least until whatever happened to drive everyone away, leaving New York City eerie and empty.

He thought about Allaire's motivations and felt sad and confused. As genuine as her love for Kyle had felt, she and Everett were married and she'd conveniently left this fact out of all of their conversations. For all he knew, the two of them planned the charade with the video of Kyle and the tattoo in advance and hired an actor to play him. Plus, this was 2060. They had all sorts of technology he couldn't understand. He wondered what was more logical: staying young forever, or Allaire and Everett trying to trick him into thinking he was someone special so they could use him to get to this Ayers character? *She lied once,* he thought. *She'll keep lying.*

A few minutes later, the pillar stopped and hovered a few feet above a building. Kyle undid his seat belt and leaned his chair back so he could access the back of the seat next to him. He flipped open the glove compartment where Allaire had left her silk blot and reached inside. He moved his hand around, but didn't feel anything. He got out of his seat to look. *When had she taken the silk blot out?* he wondered. Kyle felt himself start to panic.

He eyed the console of the pillar, looking for something. A button. An extra storage area. Some kind of answer to his problem. He climbed over the second row of seats, where he'd sat earlier, and made his way to the pillar's tail.

The aircraft got thinner the further back he went, with mostly cargo storage in the back. "Dammit!" he screamed, pounding his fist against the ceiling of the pillar in frustration. He nearly hit one of the little red fire alarm boxes.

He flipped open the other glove compartment, on the back of the pilot's seat and looked through all of the rest of the storage areas on the pillar. The very real possibility of being stuck was staring him in the face. Whether he went back to Everett and Allaire, or tried to go it alone here in 2060, he would never get to live in his own time again, and worse, never get another chance to save those kids.

It was the third time he looked at them that Kyle paid enough attention to read the little print on one of the little red fire alarm boxes. "EMERGENCY ONLY. SINGLE USE. USE WITHIN FIVE MINUTES."

It seemed strange to Kyle that four fire alarm boxes would be within a few feet of each other on a ship like the pillar, and what did "USE WITHIN FIVE MINUTES" mean? He took the metal hammer clipped to the side of one of the little boxes and broke the plastic cover. He reached his fingers inside, careful to avoid cutting himself on the sharp plastic, and pulled out the object inside which was rolled up like a taquito. When he unfurled it, he knew immediately that it was a small silk blot.

Relieved, Kyle was about to duck inside when he thought about the pillar. Allaire's silo was so isolated, so closed off from the rest of 2060 New York. She'd mentioned that it was too dangerous to leave. He wondered if she and Everett would have any safe way to even get outside without the vehicle.

Kyle went to the history menu on the auto pilot, and again keyed in the next-to-last address—the silo. He pressed "DEPLOY" to send the pillar back home, and immediately felt the thrusters kick in. He saw the door begin to slide shut, but Kyle raced to the opening and stuck his foot inside to block it, barely making it in time to prevent the door from closing. The pillar was about ten feet off the ground and rising. Kyle braced himself and jumped.

He stuck the landing like a gymnast, except for the fact that he came down only inches from the edge of the building's roof. He hit the ground and skidded forward. He needed to brace himself against the short lip rising up from the edge of the roof to avoid tumbling over. His right hand bent further backward than it was supposed to and pain shot up Kyle's arm.

He sat on the roof grimacing and holding his

wrist, thinking it might be broken. The building was tall, and he could see several blocks to his right and left. He took in this dark version of the city and wondered again what had happened to make it feel so isolated. Kyle squeezed his wrist with his hand, hoping the pain would pass, but he could already feel it swelling.

From what he gathered from the tidbits Allaire was willing to share, someone named Ayers was using the time tunnel in ways he was not supposed to. Perhaps there were others. Perhaps it was Allaire herself, or Everett, who was doing things to upset the timestream. All Kyle could do was add each of the remarkable things he observed to a list of parts which didn't yet add up to a whole.

He winced from the pain shooting through his wrist as he pulled the silk blot open. The emergency blot was more rigid and smaller than the ones he'd used before. Kyle felt both a sense of guilt and relief as he squeezed himself through and entered the time tunnel, leaving 2060 behind.

CHAPTER 16

KYLE WAS TIRED OF HIS OWN INNER MONOLOGUE after his trip through the time tunnel. It felt like it had been close to a half-day of climbing, with only his amazingly confused thoughts to keep him company. Incredibly, within minutes of entering the silk blot, his wrist felt completely healed. He had no idea if the injury had been less severe than he originally thought it was, or whether the time tunnel had somehow healed him.

He exited the tunnel and shielded his eyes from the morning sunlight. He was on top of the same building he'd stood on in 2060. He walked to a half-sized door jutting up from the roof and pulled it, but it was locked. The door was wooden, not especially sturdy and only came up to about Kyle's stomach. In no mood for any further obstacles, Kyle lifted his leg and then jabbed with the bottom of his shoe right near the knob. Four kicks later, the flimsy door swung open and Kyle ducked into a dark staircase.

A hum filled the air and got louder and louder as Kyle walked down the stairs. He found himself in a large room with at least ten industrial HVAC fans roaring around him.

He walked past the deafening fans and through a short hallway, unremarkable except for the fact that it was incredibly hot. It led to another large room, with smaller rooms off to the side. In the large room were three pieces of machinery that looked unfamiliar to Kyle.

One machine was some kind of textile contraption spinning a flat piece of material in a circle over and over again. Kyle moved closer to get a better look and he could see the material almost bubbling from the heat created as it spun faster and faster. The machine itself looked like a relic of an old factory with discolored metal, and steampunk-style levers and dials. And the heat coming off it made it almost impossible to stand near it for very long.

Kyle noticed the back of a man's bald head in one of the small rooms to the side. The rooms had a glass partition between them, and Kyle could see that the man was writing something down in a notebook.

When the man turned around, Kyle ducked behind the big spinning machine, careful not to touch the hot metal. After a few minutes Kyle stood up and peeked toward the other room, checking to see if his path to the stairwell was clear.

Kyle almost jumped out of his shoes when he saw the man standing right on the other side of the machine looking at him. The short, older man barely even flinched. "Hello," he said. He wore a three-piece brown suit and had deep olive skin and a dark goatee.

"Uh . . . Hi," Kyle answered.

The man walked around the machine toward Kyle. "I'm Yalé."

"I'm just trying to leave. I'm very sorry," Kyle said, even though the man didn't look particularly annoyed by his presence.

"It's quite alright," Yalé said. He had piercing eyes, but kept on a warm smile. "The elevator's just over there. Yalé pointed past the large room they were standing in to a small alcove just outside.

Kyle looked at the big metal machine, and the piece of fabric spinning on it. "Is that a silk blot?"

Yalé looked at Kyle and smiled again. "I wish you a good day."

Kyle headed off, but looked back once before entering the tiny elevator. He saw Yalé standing in the same place, next to the largest of the three machines, boring his eyes into Kyle. Without ever letting the smile drop off of his face, Kyle felt like Yalé had made it clear that he shouldn't come back here.

When the elevator opened on the ground floor, Kyle burst out of the building into the overcast air and headed toward the Port Authority Bus Terminal. He could be in Flemming less than six hours from now if he caught the ten a.m. bus. If there was any hope of stopping the bus crash tomorrow once and for all, he would need to set his plan in motion this evening. He kept thinking about the man in the factory, though. *Who was he? Was he the person Allaire worked for?*

CHAPTER 17

JUST AS HE HAD THE FIRST TIME HE'D TIME weaved, Kyle was able to steal the Revolutionary War era pistol from a display case above the entrance to the Flemming Central Library.

By the time Kyle had stolen the gun and gotten all of the supplies he needed, it was nearly ten in the evening on the night before the bus crash. Kyle got some restless sleep in the field behind Silverman High School and headed toward the bus driver's house at about four in the morning. The quiet street was eerily calm, and Kyle found Bus #17 parked in front of a small blue house.

For all of its massive influence on his life, Kyle had never actually seen the bus up close before. It was dredged up from Banditt Bay in the aftermath of the crash, but Kyle was in police custody by then. He walked around the bus, tracing the black ribbing in the metal along its side with his finger. He second guessed his plan for a moment. *What if I just steal the bus and hide it until tomorrow?* he wondered. But that would leave everyone's fate out of his hands. This time, if the universe was going to come to demand the lives of these twelve kids, it was going to have to go through Kyle to do it.

He glanced at the driver's house and saw that the lights were off. The street was clear, so he walked up to the back door of the bus and, quietly as he could, pulled the black handle downward, hoping Bruno had left it unlocked. Kyle pulled on the door, but it didn't budge. Then, he tiptoed around to the driver's side door, tried that, and it was also locked.

Walking back around to the rear of the vehicle, Kyle took off his backpack and unzipped it. Moments later, he jammed a crowbar into the back door and applied pressure, pulling the handle down with his other hand. He leaned into it trying to get the door to budge.

When the crowbar started to bend, Kyle became worried that the lock was too strong. He heard the metal of the door straining against the leverage he applied with the crowbar, but it held firm over a few minutes during which Kyle tried a few different angles, and a few different pivot points on the door.

Just as he was about to give up and move to Plan B, breaking a window, he got the door to lurch open. Kyle tossed his backpack inside and climbed in. He jammed himself between the back seat and the seatback in front of it in order to stay hidden for as long as possible. If Kyle had his way, Bruno would make all of his morning pickups before anyone even knew he was on the bus. Unlikely, but the longer he stayed hidden, the better.

Kyle opened his eyes and lifted his head off of the green plastic seat of the bus when he heard the back door slam closed. He jumped as the door swung against the frame, and then bounced open again.

"Who're you?" Bruno yelled at him from outside the bus, making eye contact. "Get outta my bus!"

Kyle quickly opened his backpack and put on his ski mask. He pointed the pistol at Bruno. "I don't want to hurt anyone, but I need to come with you today on your pickups."

Bruno stepped back, putting his hands up. He looked toward his house.

"Don't get your wife involved, Mr. Pasquale," Kyle said. "I don't want anyone getting hurt."

"You broke my bus," Bruno said.

Kyle could see now that the latch where the lock was supposed to catch was a mess of bent metal. "I'm sorry about that."

"How am I gonna drive?" Bruno asked.

"I'll hold it for now, and then one of the kids can help," Kyle answered.

"You wanna someone tumble out the back?" Bruno asked, getting agitated now.

Kyle waved his pistol toward the front of the bus. "I don't want anybody to get hurt, Mr. Pasquale. I promise. I just need you to treat today like any other morning pickup."

Bruno talked animatedly with his hands now. "Treat it like every other morning? I don't have a guy with a gun on my bus most mornings—"

"No, you don't," Kyle said. "But, like I said, I need you to trust me. If you do, nobody will get hurt. Now, please, let's go start the pickups."

Bruno shook his head and muttered to himself, but eventually, he walked around to the driver's side door. He opened it and pulled himself up onto the seat. He looked at Kyle angrily through the huge rear-view mirror. "What you want anyway?"

"Would you believe I'm here to keep you and the children safe?" Kyle asked. But the older man just waved at the air and started the ignition. Kyle knelt in the aisle and held the back door closed by its handle.

Bruno didn't say another word until just before they got to the first house on the route. They were on the outskirts of Flemming. He continued to hold tightly onto the door, making sure it didn't fly open as Bruno drove.

"Why don't we leave the kids outta this? I take you wherever you need," Bruno said, as he pulled up in front of Marlon Peters' house.

"Honk the horn, Mr. Pasquale," Kyle said, raising the antique pistol into the air to remind him one last time who was in charge here.

Moments later, Marlon Peters lumbered up the steps and onto the bus. Marlon stood in the center aisle and looked at Kyle, still wearing a ski mask.

Kyle could see the mixture of curiosity and alarm in the kid's expression.

"Come here, kid," Kyle said. He had to stop himself from calling Marlon by his name.

Marlon looked back at Bruno, who was watching through the rear view as he drove. Then, he stepped toward Kyle, still keeping a few feet between them.

"Can you do me a favor?" Kyle asked. "My name is Frank, and I need some help with this door. Can you sit back here and hold it shut for me?"

Marlon cautiously sat in the back seat and put his hand on the door handle, pulling it completely closed. "It's not my seat," he mumbled.

"Today it is, kid," Kyle answered.

The story Kyle told each of the kids as they boarded the bus was that he worked for the bus company and was observing the run so he could substitute for Bruno if necessary. To a man, each kid questioned him about the ski mask, and after several bad excuses, Kyle told all of them that he'd been burned badly in an accident and preferred wearing a mask to scaring people.

The final pickup was Serg Sidorov. After he bounded up the stairs and took his seat, Bruno closed the front door of the bus and looked back through the rearview. He gave the universal "what now?" gesture to Kyle.

Kyle looked at his watch. "Sixteen Thirty-two Wolkoff Parkway," he called up to him.

Marlon had lost hold of the door a few times, meaning they had to stop the bus and someone had to get out and close it. Now that all of the kids were on the bus, and sooner or later they'd realize that they weren't headed to school. Kyle needed someone back there he could trust.

The morning conversations between the kids were loud. Marlon had been right, Etan Rachnowitz was none too thrilled to see a sixth grader in his back row seat. It was surreal to Kyle to be amongst these kids who he only knew through newspaper clippings.

He knew, for instance, that Tiffany Preston and Lisa Cartigliani were not the demure, quiet types, but seeing them bark out disses like they were on a construction crew was more than Kyle could process. He looked around at all of them— these living, breathing kids—and felt a surge of happiness. Sitting here with these children who had only been ghosts to him made Kyle feel, for the first time since the original crash, like his slate was clean. Even if this only lasted a few more minutes, Kyle could barely contain his giddiness. *They're all alive*, he thought.

He thought about the possibility of the bus crashing this morning with him on it. It would be a poetic ending for him, especially since these last moments were giving him such joy.

A few minutes later, the bus pulled up in front of Kyle's house. So he could avoid getting out so close to his 2014 self, he asked Bruno to pull up on the lawn. Kyle had him drive around the side of the house, damaging his mother's plants in the process. He scanned the yard and after a few minutes, he saw a pair of shoes sticking out from a hedge.

Kyle slid down one of the windows on the bus. "Sillow!" he yell-whispered to his father, who was at his house fulfilling a promise he'd made to Kyle in 1998 to try to stop the original crash.

Sillow peeked above the bushes with a confused look. Kyle lifted the mask for a quick second, and waved him toward the bus. "Let him in please, Bruno."

As soon as Sillow walked up the stairs into the bus, Kyle tossed him a ski mask. Sillow looked at it for a second, shrugged, and then put it on.

"His face ain't burned," Lisa Cartigliani yelled to no one in particular. "Who the fuck is this guy? And why's he gettin' a mask?"

"Yeah," Jim Henderson said. "Who are you guys anyway?"

Tom Snodgrass looked up from his Star Trek book. "Could you both shut the hell up? Who cares who they are as long as we get to school?"

"Bruno, drive please," Kyle called up.

"Where?" Bruno asked, sounding irritated.

Kyle leaned down to Bruno's ear and gave him directions. Then, he walked to the back of the bus and tugged on Sillow's jacket to pull him in close. "I know I asked you to do something different sixteen years ago," he whispered. "But it turns out that what I really need is for you to just hold this back door closed. Don't let any of these kids get past you. No matter what."

Scarlett Finch hadn't cared too much about the guys with the masks until they insisted on taking her iPod. She tried explaining that it wasn't a phone, but the main guy didn't care. He said she'd get it back later as he made her dump it into the plastic bag.

At first he was nice about the whole thing, but when Etan told him he wouldn't give up his iPhone, the guy pulled out an old looking gun and shoved it in his face. "That's a whack-ass piece," Etan said, unwilling to show that he was scared. Still, he turned off his phone and handed it over a second later.

Once he had a device from every kid except Tom, who managed to convince him he didn't have one, the main guy whispered something to Bruno and switched places with him, sitting down in the driver's seat. Bruno silently sat down next to Marlon.

The bus got quieter after the guy threatened Etan. It was the first time in a long while that the ever-present yapping of the eighth graders didn't drown out every other noise on the bus.

Everything stayed quiet for a couple of hours, all of the kids whispering to their seatmates about what might be going on. They were heading up the New York State Thruway going further and further north.

"Hey, Mister," Tiffany called up to the front. "Where the hell are you taking us?" The immediate shock of watching the man threaten Etan with his gun had faded a bit. By now, Scarlett felt like everyone must be getting as antsy as she was. She also wondered if her bus-mates had come to the same conclusion she had. If these guys wanted to kill them, they were certainly going far out of their way to do it. Something in the way the two guys in ski masks acted toward the kids told Scarlett that they weren't people who intended to hurt them.

"Are you gonna sew us together, mouth to ass, like in that movie *Human Centipede*?" Etan called up, not quite sounding like his confident self, but cockier than Scarlett would've been if she'd had a gun shoved in her face a few hours ago.

The driver just ignored the kids and drove,

keeping a slow pace in the right lane. Kind of the way Scarlett's grandmother drove the Thruway. It went on that way for almost an hour. The loudmouths on the Cheese Bus shouting at the driver, or trying to get the guy holding the door to talk. But both of the guys in the masks just kept silent.

CHAPTER 18

"WHERE ARE YOU GOING?" SCARLETT ASKED Patty as she stood up from her window seat and brushed past her. By now, all of the kids were aware that the bus wasn't heading to school today.

The guy in the ski mask who was driving had assured them that they'd be home by later in the evening and that he didn't want to hurt anyone. The further north they drove, the more remote the chance of getting home by that evening became. It was nearly three in the afternoon—the end of the school day.

Scarlett watched, confused, as Patty walked to the back of the bus. She had been trying to get the driver's attention for a few minutes, but Patty was so soft-spoken, and Scarlett was way too intimidated by him to speak up on her behalf.

Scarlett turned around, knees on the seat, and watched Patty walk up to the guy holding the door closed. He sat in the back seat, looking out the back window. He didn't turn at first, but she just stood over him. Scarlett couldn't hear what she was saying, but eventually he looked up at her.

"Hey," the guy in the back called to "Frank," the guy driving, "She says she's gotta pee real bad."

"Fifteen minutes," 'Frank' said.

"She's sayin' she can't wait," he called up.

The driver shook his head. "Fifteen minutes. Sorry."

Tom Snodgrass stood up, leaving his book on the seat. He was the biggest kid on the bus. Definitely the most physically imposing. "Hey driver," Tom said. "Are you deaf? Stop the fucking bus."

But the driver didn't respond. Tom looked forward and saw that the driver wasn't even looking back at them. Scarlett could see the wheels churning in his head. He grabbed the guy holding the door in the back by his shirt collar and started pushing him out.

"This is some bullshit," Tom called up to the driver. "It's time for some answers, and it's time for you to pull this fucking bus over."

The door to the back of the bus swung open as the guy in the ski mask braced both arms against the doorframe trying to keep himself inside. A fall from a moving bus onto the busy Thruway would mean certain death.

CHAPTER 19

MARCH 13, 2014

moments later

KYLE STARTED TO LOSE CONTROL OF THE BUS AS soon as he saw the door swing open, and the scene in the back with Sillow trying to stop Tom Snodgrass from pushing him out the door.

"Stop!" Kyle yelled, trying to straighten himself out as he rolled over the white lines on each side of the middle lane. "I'll stop the bus. I'll stop. Just give me a second to pull off!"

He watched as Tom backed off from Sillow for a second, stepping behind Patty Marshall. Sillow looked like he was trying to catch his breath. Then, he suddenly reared back and threw a punch toward Tom, who dodged out of the way.

This was the first unusual behavior Kyle had seen from his father since they'd met in 1998. Kyle couldn't understand how his dad had managed to be such a deadbeat. All Kyle had found, once he got past Sillow's initial gruff behavior, was someone willing to help him in this crazy scenario, and trying to make amends. He'd found everything he could want from a father, minus the shared history.

Kyle got himself into the right lane and started slowing his speed down, preparing to pull onto the side of the road, but it was too narrow to pull off on this stretch of the Thruway.

"I'm gonna stop as soon as I have a shoulder," Kyle yelled toward the back. "Just calm down and hold tight."

Tom was grabbing Sillow now, and trying to land a punch to his face. Kyle tried to keep an eye on the road, but couldn't help but watch what was going on behind him. Suddenly, as Tom and Sillow pushed and grabbed each other—each trying to get the upper hand—Kyle heard Tiffany scream, "Patty!"

Patty Marshall had been pushed out during the scuffle and was now clinging onto the back door to save herself from falling onto the Thruway. Kyle was afraid to jam on the breaks and jar her off the door. He knew the drastic impact Patty's death in the original bus crash had on her family. Her father wound up in rehab for a drinking problem he'd never had before, and her mother showed up at Kyle's trial each day in pajamas. Kyle knew each of these kids so deeply and richly that the pressure to keep them safe now, and the worry that he might not be able to, gave him a hollow feeling deep in his stomach.

Tom and Sillow stopped fighting and moved quickly toward the doorway. Kyle only had a partial view through the rearview, so he took his eyes off the road for a second and turned around. *This is exactly what time wants,* he thought, *a way to get this bus into a dangerous situation where something can kill these twelve kids.* With this thought knocking around in his head like a pinball, he looked up and saw Sillow holding Tom by the waist as Tom reached out his hand toward Patty. The seventh grader was hugging the top and side of the back door like a boogie board.

Kyle could hear Patty screaming and was relieved to see a widening shoulder up ahead about fifty yards. He slowed down and put on his turn signal. He rolled over the gravel and tried to stop as gently as he could. He heard the door swing shut as he stopped. By then, though, Sillow and Tom had pulled Patty back inside the bus. Tears streamed from her eyes and Tom patted her on the back.

Kyle stood up and opened the door of the bus. He didn't see the harm in letting them stretch their legs, so he told them they could get out for a few minutes. As he exited the bus, Sillow looked up at Kyle, who shook his head in amazement. Kyle couldn't believe his father would be stupid enough to get into a fist fight with an eighth grader.

"Just playing defense," Sillow said. "He almost killed me."

Kyle rolled his eyes. "He's like, thirteen."

It was starting to get dark. The time of the original crash had passed hours ago and the kids were all still alive. Kyle wouldn't feel confident, though, that he'd changed anything for good until March 13 had come and gone, which meant keeping these kids another six hours. Allaire had told him there was no chance of getting these kids to March 14 alive. He had no idea what would come after, but he was only six hours from getting them through today.

Kyle wished he had somewhere safe to bring the kids for the next few hours so they weren't just driving around. He was afraid that, after all this, the universe could still manufacture a different version of the crash here on the Thruway. Everything he'd learned in these last few weeks about time travel was that the universe wanted things to stay as they were. *Six more hours.*

But, maybe . . . Maybe Joe Stropoli being far away . . . Maybe Sillow and Kyle being on the bus . . . Maybe getting the kids out of Flemming . . . Maybe this was all enough to keep them all safe *for six more hours.*

Still, Kyle wished he had the option to stop moving.

As the kids emptied out onto the wide shoulder of the road, Kyle noticed most of the students were standing in a row looking at him. They wanted some kind of explanation. Some way of understanding what they were doing here along the side of the New York State Thruway, hours away from Flemming. He needed to avoid any further unrest among them. Things were too tenuous for any more risks.

"What the hell are we doing here?" Lisa called out.

"Let's wait until Patty gets back," Kyle answered. "Anyone else who has to use the bathroom, there's bushes right back there."

"How do you know our names?" one of the

Costello twins asked him. Kyle couldn't tell which one.

"I don't," Kyle answered, lying to them. It had been a mistake to use Patty's name, but it was hard to pretend they were strangers.

Kyle was about to speak when a tan minivan pulled up directly behind the bus. It looked like it was rolling to a stop, but then Kyle saw that it actually wasn't. He got a quick look at the driver, and then screamed to the kids.

"Watch out!" Kyle yelled. "Get out of the way!"

The kids all looked up and started throwing themselves out of the way of the oncoming minivan. The vehicle barreled toward them, and then stopped briefly in the weeds beyond the shoulder before it started rolling backward. Allaire had warned Kyle that it might not be her trying to stop him next time, and it wasn't.

It was Everett behind the wheel, reversing and trying to aim for the large group of kids now standing near the bus. Everett knew exactly what

Kyle was trying to do, and determined to stop him, he attempted to run over the children.

"Look out!" Kyle screamed, running toward the group of five or six kids. He corralled them in his arms, pushing them away from the bus.

Everett's minivan smashed into the side of Bus #17 before rolling forward and into the weeds again. The kids were screaming. It was absolute chaos.

The wheels on Everett's van got stuck, and they just spun as he tried to dislodge himself from the dirt and weeds.

"Who the fuck *is* that?" Sillow shouted.

"Someone who doesn't want us messing with things," Kyle yelled back. "All of you! On to the bus!"

Kyle pushed and pulled all of the kids onto the bus as Everett spun his wheels trying to get out of the muck. Just as the door to Everett's van swung open, Kyle pushed the last kid inside and hopped into the driver's seat.

Kyle watched Everett through his side view mirror, holding a shotgun as he approached the bus. He pointed the shotgun, cocked it and fired once. "Get down!" Kyle screamed to the kids as the back window exploded. Kyle wasn't sure if anyone was hit. He threw on the ignition, but cars zipped by on the Thruway. It might take a couple of minutes to find an opportunity to merge back into traffic.

Kyle ducked his head down, looking at traffic in the side view. He could see Everett too, raising the shotgun toward the bus again. Kyle decided to open the driver's side door and hop out. He put his hands in the air and walked toward Everett. None of his time weaving had been about his own life. If it ended here for him, at least it was while he was trying to right his greatest wrong.

As he walked toward him, Kyle half expected to be blown to bits by a shotgun round right then and there.

"I don't have to kill *you*," Everett said. "Only them."

"Why?" Kyle asked.

Everett cocked the shotgun again. "Because you couldn't leave well enough alone."

"Well enough?" Kyle pleaded. "They have a chance now! Or, they would . . . "

"Who are you to say who deserves a chance?" Everett said. "There are no do-overs in life."

"Of course there are!" Kyle said. "Why would time travel exist otherwise? Why would you and Allaire try to fix the things that get messed up? Aren't those *do-overs?* These kids, they're here, Everett. You can just walk away and let them live . . . Or, let the universe decide if they live." He was standing close to Everett now.

"We both know these kids should be dead," Everett said, raising the shotgun toward Kyle. "Now, are you gonna let me do my job? Or do I need to take you down too?"

Kyle's eyes lit up when he saw the headlights of his own Nissan Sentra. The car skidded onto the shoulder, and out came Allaire. She opened the door and walked toward them with a somber look on her face.

Everett aimed the shotgun at Kyle and didn't move a muscle.

"Allaire," Kyle said. "Tell him not to kill all of these kids."

Allaire looked at Kyle, but wouldn't make eye contact.

"Please!" Kyle screamed, realizing that she wasn't there with the same agenda as his own. "Tell him to let them go."

"Those kids don't belong here," Allaire said, pulling out her pistol. "They don't have a place in the world anymore. They're a glitch."

"What are you talking about?" Kyle asked. "This is crazy! They're right here. Living and breathing."

Allaire walked up closer to Everett, who had his gun trained on the bus now. She whispered something to him.

When she looked at Kyle, he could see that her eyes were filled with tears. "I'm sorry."

Everett started pumping shotgun rounds into the bus as quickly as he could reload the double barrel weapon. The first two shots slammed against, and through, the metal of the bus like they were cannonballs.

Kyle was thrilled to hear the engine of the bus kick back on. He'd told Bruno to take the bus and just go if he heard any gunshots.

Everett reloaded another two rounds into the shotgun as Bruno turned the bus toward the Thruway. All he had to do was find a clear space to merge, but traffic wasn't cooperating as car after car raced by. Kyle saw the back door swing open and his stomach dropped. He wondered if Sillow had been hit by one of the rounds Everett fired at the bus again.

Kyle needed to give the bus a few seconds to get off on its way. He lowered his shoulder and charged at Everett. It only took a fling of Everett's forearm, though, to push Kyle out of the way.

As Kyle got up and came at him again, Everett

got off another shot at the bus. The horn blared, and at first, Kyle assumed it was Bruno trying to make his way off the shoulder and into traffic, but the horn didn't stop. When Kyle looked at the driver's seat, he could see Bruno's mangled half-head laying on the steering wheel. Everett had blown it clear off.

Ignoring Everett, Kyle ran toward the bus, the dirt from the Thruway shoulder kicking up beneath his feet. He could see that the students had all taken cover on the floor, clear of the windows. He heard Everett pump the shotgun again and waited for the bullet to either hit him in the back, or thud against the bus.

Kyle opened the driver's side door and pulled Bruno down from the seat, laying him down on the gravelly ground. The way Bruno's head looked reminded Kyle of Joe Stropoli on the day of the original crash.

Kyle turned around and saw that Allaire and Everett were scuffling now. She was trying to pull the shotgun away from him, while her pistol was on the ground at her feet. Kyle saw Allaire connect with a roundhouse kick, which knocked Everett to the ground. Her moves looked like something out of a movie, but in real life, a kick like that one was enough to fell anyone, even a big guy like Everett.

Allaire knelt next to Everett and unloaded with three punches to the head, one after the other.

Kyle grabbed Bruno's ankles and pulled him away so he wouldn't run over him. He looked up at Allaire and saw her pick up the shotgun.

Kyle couldn't get the words out quickly enough to warn her before Everett grabbed her ankle and pulled her to the ground. She slid on the dirt and fell face first, the shotgun coming to rest directly underneath her.

Everett violently pulled the shotgun out and butted her in the forehead. The blow sent Allaire's head snapping back into the ground. She wasn't knocked out, but it was enough to incapacitate her for the moment. Everett cocked the gun and pointed it down at Allaire, then up at the bus. Kyle looked backward and tried to line himself up between the barrel of the gun and the bus.

"I didn't need to kill you," Everett said, aiming at Kyle now. "Dummy."

Kyle winced, ready for the kill shot. He had the thought for a brief instant that he was about to die for nothing, since Everett would just march past his dead body and murder every kid on the bus to keep with what he believed the universe wanted.

Then, Kyle heard the gravel behind him moving. He looked back and saw Sillow at the wheel of the bus. He'd turned the bus ever so slightly, about to merge into traffic.

Everett no longer had a clear shot into the driver's seat. He moved closer to the oncoming traffic for a better angle and fired once. As Everett aimed at the bus's tires, Kyle moved so he was in the way of his shots. He'd have to shoot Kyle to shoot the bus again. Everett aimed at Kyle's chest and cocked the weapon.

Kyle saw what Everett was too busy to notice. Allaire charged at him like a linebacker in pursuit. She ran into him and sent him off balance. He stumbled to his left and stepped over the white line dividing the shoulder and the right lane of the Thruway. Kyle noticed a look of panic on his face when Everett noticed he was on the asphalt instead of the gravelly shoulder.

Seconds later, Everett was hit hard by a maroon Volvo, the collision sending him flying fifteen feet into the weeds beyond the shoulder.

By the time Kyle could register what had happened, the bus was gone. Kyle could hardly believe that they'd survived the threat from Everett and would soon be heading back toward Flemming. If Sillow could keep them safe during the ride back, it would be after midnight when they arrived home and the kids would have lived to see March 14.

Allaire walked over to Everett's body in the weeds, and knelt next to him. The look on her face was solemn, but not devastated. Kyle pulled off his ski mask but gave her a few feet of distance. They'd have to get out of here soon so neither of them ended up in police custody here in 2014. Someone would've definitely called the police when they saw a man on the side of the Thruway pointing a shotgun at a school bus.

"One thing," Allaire said, kneeling next to Everett and closing his eyes.

"What?" Kyle asked, stepping a little closer.

"He gave his life to one thing," she said. "And he failed. *We* failed."

Kyle walked around Everett's body so he could see Allaire's face. "Allaire, I know you think that this is going to mess up the whole universe—"

"I don't *think* it will, Kyle. It will. I do this every, single day. Keeping the timestream safe *is* my life. You ever hear of President Kardashian?"

"No," Kyle answered.

"What about the A-Bomb Destruction of Houston, or the Global Small Pox Plague of 1989?" she asked.

Kyle looked at her, confused. "No. Of course not."

"That's because we never allowed those things to happen," she said. "You might not see it today. Or tomorrow. Or even when you go back to 2016. But those kids being alive throws off a very delicate balance. Twelve lives magically reappearing in the universe could throw things into exactly the kind of chaos that Ayers wants." She put her hand on Everett's chest and spoke lower now. "He'll do more things too. Sometimes we win, and sometimes he does. But Ayers will just keep playing with the timestream until it's the end of us all."

She stood up and walked closer to Kyle now. Other than the dead bodies, they were alone now on the side of the Thruway, a light breeze kicking up at their feet. She was close enough for him to kiss her. "You know the saying, 'you're either part of the solution, or part of the problem'?"

He nodded.

"When you took that pillar, we needed you," Allaire said. "Seeing that you hadn't aged means you might be the key to stopping Ayers—the key to mankind's future—and you bailed. And the worst part is that you did it to save yourself. You make it about the kids, when it's really all about you." Kyle didn't agree with her characterization, but that was a fight for another time.

"Did I fall in love with you fast?" she asked. "Sure. But, I assumed that the Kyle I knew would be there when the shit hit the fan. That you were the kind of person that would step up."

"I am," he said. "I want to be."

She gave him a subtle look that he'd never seen before, but he knew it just the same. Her feelings for him had been to the mountaintop, but they'd fallen, and they weren't likely to come back. "You're not, Kyle Cash. I wanted to believe you were. I *needed* to believe you were the hero that was going to make everything right. But the proof is in that bus. You couldn't just have faith and do what I asked." Her words trailed off, as tears fell from her eyes.

"But . . . "

Allaire turned away from him, and then reached into her pocket. She flipped him the keys to his Sentra. "You should get back. There's a blot sitting on the passenger seat. If those kids survive another few hours, you'll be a free man in 2016. Congratulations."

"What about you?" Kyle asked.

"I'll be cleaning up the mess," she said.

"Let me help you," Kyle said.

"Just go, please," Allaire answered

"I want to make this right," Kyle said.

"It's too late," Allaire answered. "You can't! Just go, please. Before the police come. Go back and live your life outside of a jail cell."

That he'd managed to fall so far in her eyes, so quickly, made Kyle feel a deep and dark sense of regret, completely squashing his excitement over getting the kids of Bus #17 to likely safety. He walked away with his head hanging, got into his Sentra and pulled onto the Thruway.

CHAPTER 20

MARCH 14, 2014

just after midnight

As Kyle pressed his ear to the payphone, he listened to it ring three times and assumed it would go to voicemail. But, then, a groggy voice answered. "Heh—Hello??"

"Is your brother at home?" Kyle asked, pressing a finger into his other ear to block out the music blaring through the gas station.

"My brother?" the voice answered. "Do you have any idea what time it is?"

Kyle looked across the street at the digital display on the sign of another gas station. "Yes, Myrna. It's about a quarter past midnight."

He'd realized that he could enter the silk blot

sitting in his car from anywhere. For every 'rule' of time weaving Kyle learned, it seemed like he learned an exception too. Before going back to 2016, Kyle needed to know that the kids had made it back, so he'd killed some time waiting around a Thruway gas station.

"Who is this?" Myrna asked, sounding panicked. "Were you involved with what happened today?" If everything turned out differently, there'd never be a need for Myrna and Kyle to know each other. "Mom! Pick up the phone. I think it's the guy who kidnapped Etan today."

"Please," Kyle said. "Just tell me if he made it home."

Kyle heard the click of another phone picking up. "Is it really you?" the voice of a young kid answered. "Suck it, you cock knocker! Your gun was the saddest looking piece of shit I've ever seen, you poor mutherfucker." Kyle smiled knowing that Etan was home, safe and sound.

He hung up the phone, and headed back to his car, ready to head into a silk blot one last time.

CHAPTER 21

FEBRUARY 25, 2016

two years later

KYLE HEADED DOWN MAIN STREET IN FLEMMING. He couldn't wait to see his mother alive later when she got home from work. He couldn't wait to sleep in his bed. To decide what he'd do for once, instead of being told.

He knew he'd probably never see Allaire again and that his life as a time weaver would soon be a distant memory. He'd let her down, but in the end, he was right. He'd stopped the crash, and the world seemed just fine.

So fine that, when Kyle passed the Starbucks on Main Street, he ducked inside for a celebratory drink. The idea of a vanilla bean frappuccino made his mouth water. He couldn't remember the last time he'd done something just for the enjoyment of it. He checked his back pocket, found a couple of twenty dollar bills and headed inside.

A little while later, he strolled toward his house drinking his frappuccino. It was four in the afternoon, so he still had another hour until his mom would be home. She'd think it'd been only hours since they'd seen each other.

As he walked, Kyle felt intoxicated by his new-found freedom. Those kids would get to live normal, unabbreviated lives now, and he had a chance to pick up where he left off. Still, Allaire managed to creep into his thoughts too.

She'd told him she thought he might be the one who could help them make everything right. *But, what was more right than giving life to the kids from the bus?* Kyle wondered. She'd wanted Kyle to be a hero, but by going against what she asked of him, he felt like one. It was hard for Kyle to believe, at the moment, that there was anything wrong with the world at all, much less that he'd need to keep time weaving to help fix it.

It was a beautiful day, so Kyle decided to meander until his mom got home. He walked down Nairn Boulevard toward the high school sucking on his frappuccino. Perhaps he could steal a nap in the same grassy field where he and Allaire had spent the night together all the way back in 1998. *Life is good*, Kyle thought. *The universe is fine just as it is.*

When he came within about a half block of Silverman High, though, he noticed that something looked different. The building wasn't where it was supposed to be. He hadn't been in prison so long that he'd forgotten where the school was. *What was going on?* he wondered to himself.

Kyle ran down the block now and stood across the street from where the school had been. He waited for the cars to pass as he scanned the area in front of him. The grass was still there, but it was more expansive now. There was no school building anywhere in sight. It looked just like a park. He felt a strange sensation in his stomach, like someone had just punched him. His brain was flooded with memories, but there were too many hitting him at once to make any sense of them.

Kyle ran through the grass and felt disoriented. What used to be a school, surrounded by a large field of grass was now just a field. No signs. Nothing. "What the hell?" He wondered aloud.

He ran in to the convenience store across the street and walked up to the counter where an older man in a white t-shirt sat on a stool with a cigar hanging out of his mouth. Kyle was out of breath, puffing and huffing as he spoke.

"Where's the high school?" Kyle asked, pointing across the street. "The school! It used to be, I mean, it was right here."

"What?" the man asked, scrunching up his face.

"The school! Silverman High!" Kyle said tersely. "Where'd it go?"

"I don't like your tone, kid," the guy said, standing up from his stool. He put his cigar in an ashtray, and Kyle was afraid he was going to come out from behind the counter.

Kyle put his hands in front of him to try to calm the guy down. "Listen, I'm sorry. I just . . . I just really don't know . . . where the school went. I'm not from around here."

"No shit, you're not," the guy said, "You've gotta be from Mars or somethin' not to know what happened," the store clerk said, shaking his head in disbelief. "It was over a year ago. This little girl. She wired the whole school with C4. Poof. Took out over three hundred kids and about forty teachers. They tore down the little bit that was left a few months ago. You ask me, those kids deserve more of a memorial than a damn field."

Kyle's knees started to shake as his legs felt weaker and weaker every second.

The store clerk turned around and unpinned an article from the wall behind him. "You ever read a newspaper before? Here. Knock yourself out. Read all about it." The clerk placed the article on the counter.

Kyle picked up the clipping. His hands felt shaky as he scanned the article. He couldn't help his gag reflex when he read the name of the bomber. He threw up right on the tile floor in front of the counter.

"What the hell are you doing?" the clerk asked.

Kyle stumbled out of the store and looked across the street to the former site of the school. In a million years he wouldn't have guessed Lisa Cartigliani could be capable of something like this. The world felt to him like it was spinning too fast and Kyle couldn't keep his balance.

He fell to his knees. More than three hundred children dead. Forty teachers. All because he'd gone back and saved twelve lives. Allaire had been right after all.

Kyle buried his face in his hands and screamed.

To be continued . . .